Dedalus European Class[...]
Editor: Mike Mitchell

Alves & Co.
and Other Stories

Eça de Queiroz

Alves & Co.
and Other Stories

Dedalus

Funded by the Direcção-Geral do Livro das Bibliotecas/Portugal

Supported using public funding by
ARTS COUNCIL
ENGLAND

Published in the UK by Dedalus Limited,
24-26, St Judith's Lane, Sawtry, Cambs, PE28 5XE
email: info@dedalusbooks.com
www.dedalusbooks.com

ISBN 978 1 903517 89 5

Dedalus is distributed in the USA and Canada by SCB Distributors,
15608 South New Century Drive, Gardena, CA 90248
email: info@scbdistributors.com   web: www.scbdistributors.com

Dedalus is distributed in Australia by Peribo Pty Ltd.
58, Beaumont Road, Mount Kuring-gai, N.S.W. 2080
email: info@peribo.com.au

Publishing History
First Published in Portugal in 1880/1925
First published by Dedalus in 2012

Translation copyright © Margaret Jull Costa 2012

The right of Margaret Jull Costa to be identified as the translator of this
work has been asserted by her in accordance with the Copyright, Designs
and Patents Act, 1988.

Printed in Finland by Bookwell
Typeset by Marie Lane

The Translator

Margaret Jull Costa has translated the work of many Spanish and Portuguese writers, amongst them Rafael Sánchez Ferlosio, Ramón del Valle-Inclán, José Régio and Mário de Sá-Carneiro.

She was awarded the 1992 Portuguese Translation Prize for *The Book of Disquiet* by Fernando Pessoa. With Javier Marías, she won the translator's portion of the 1997 International IMPAC Dublin Literary Award for *A Heart So White*.

In 2000, she won the Weidenfeld Translation Prize for José Saramago's All the Names and in 2006, won the Premio Valle-Inclán for *Your Face Tomorrow: I Fever and Spear* by Javier Marías. Her translation of Eça's *The Maias* brought her the 2008 PEN/Book-of-the-Month Club Translation Prize and the 2008 Oxford-Weidenfeld Translation Prize.

She has since won the 2010 and 2011 Premio Valle-Inclán for, respectively, Bernardo Atxaga's *The Accordionist's Son* and volume three of Javier Marías' trilogy, *Your Face Tomorrow*, and the 2011 Oxford-Weidenfeld Translation Prize for *The Elephant's Journey* by José Saramago.

Contents

Introduction

José Maria de Eça de Queiroz was born on 25th November 1845 in the small town of Póvoa de Varzim in the north of Portugal. His mother was nineteen and unmarried. Only the name of his father – a magistrate – appears on the birth certificate. Following the birth, his mother returned immediately to her respectable family in Viana do Castelo, and Eça was left with his wet nurse, who looked after him for six years until her death. Although his parents married later – when Eça was four – and had six more children, Eça did not live with them until he was twenty-one, living instead either with his grandparents or at boarding school in Oporto, where he spent the holidays with an aunt. His father only officially acknowledged Eça as his son when the latter was forty. He did, however, pay for his son's studies at boarding school and at Coimbra University, and was always supportive of his writing ambitions. After working as the editor and sole contributor on a provincial newspaper in Évora, Eça made a trip to the Middle East. Then, in order to launch himself on a diplomatic career, he worked for six months in Leiria, a provincial town north of Lisbon, as a municipal administrator, before being appointed consul in Havana (1872–74), Newcastle-upon-Tyne (1874–79) and Bristol (1879–88). In 1886, he married Emília de Castro with whom he had four children. His last consular posting was to Paris in 1888. He served there until his death in 1900 at the age of only 54.

He began writing stories and essays as a young man and became involved with a group of intellectuals known as the

Generation of '70, who were committed to reforms in society and in the arts. He published four novels and one novella during his lifetime: *The Crime of Father Amaro* (3 versions: 1875, 1876, 1880), *Cousin Bazilio* (1878), *The Mandarin* (1880), *The Relic* (1887) and *The Maias* (1888). His other fiction was published posthumously: *The City and the Mountains*, *The Illustrious House of Ramires*, *To the Capital*, *Alves & Co.*, *The Letters of Fradique Mendes*, *The Count of Abranhos* and *The Tragedy of the Street of Flowers*.

Like that other great Portuguese writer, Fernando Pessoa, Eça left behind a large trunk containing all his unpublished work. *Alves & Co.* was one of those manuscripts. It was probably written around 1883, but this is by no means certain. Some critics believe that it may have been part of his projected series of novellas, "Cenas Portuguesas" or "Scenes from Portuguese Life", but no one is sure. The manuscript bore neither date nor title and, although there were corrections and changes made in Eça's hand, it was clearly not a finished version. However, his son, José Maria, carefully deciphered what he called his father's 'vertiginous' script and published it, with the title *Alves & Co.*, in 1925, twenty-five years after his father's death.

Its moral focus is very different from Eça's earlier novels – *The Crime of Father Amaro* and *Cousin Bazilio* – in which transgression has tragic consequences. In this essentially comic novella, Eça's sharp eye for the absurd is tempered by compassion and by the revolutionary thought that forgiving and forgetting might sometimes be the preferable option. He draws great humour from the situation, but also shows remarkable psychological acuity in his descriptions of the betrayed husband Godofredo's pain and confusion.

In the companion volume to this – *The Mandarin and*

Other Stories – there seemed to be a common preoccupation with reality and fantasy. Such a thread is less obvious here. 'A Lyric Poet' can be seen as another droll look at Romanticism; after all, what could be less romantic than working as a waiter in the Charing Cross Hotel? 'At the Mill' could be read partly as a homage to Flaubert and Maupassant. 'The Treasure' will be recognisable to readers of Chaucer as a variant of *The Pardoner's Tale*, which was itself based on an Oriental folk-tale. 'Brother Juniper' is a version (with a very different ending) of a story that appears in *Little Flowers of St Francis*. 'The Wet Nurse' is a medieval tale about someone who takes their loyalty to its ultimate, logical conclusion. And 'The Sweet Miracle', written for an anthology of stories published to raise money for charity, represents Eça's belief in the rightness and simplicity of Jesus's teachings as opposed to what he perceived as the Catholic Church's more worldly and hierarchical concerns.

Unlike *Alves & Co.,* the stories were all published during Eça's lifetime, the earliest – 'A Lyric Poet' and 'At the Mill' – in 1880 and the last – 'The Sweet Miracle' – in 1898.

These remarkably diverse stories illustrate Eça's ability not only to write in very different modes, but to imagine his way into different minds and psychological states; for, as well as his wonderful sense of the absurd, Eça always showed enormous insight into even the most minor of his characters. The novella and the stories are a testament to that great talent.

Alves & Co.

I

That day, Godofredo da Conceição Alves, hot and bothered and still breathless from having almost run all the way from Terreiro do Paço, was just pushing open the green baize door of his mezzanine office in Rua dos Douradores when the clock on the wall above the bookkeeper's desk struck two, the low ceilings lending a doleful sonority to the cavernous tone of the chime. Godofredo stopped, checked his own watch – which he wore attached to his white waistcoat by a chain of braided hair – and scowled. He had once again wasted the entire morning visiting the Admiralty. It made not a jot of difference that the Director-General was his wife's cousin, nor that he sometimes slipped the errand boys a tip, and had, on previous occasions, discounted bills of exchange for two minor officials, no, despite all that, there was always the same agonising wait to see the minister, the same never-ending leafing-through of paperwork, the hesitations and delays, like the fractious, creaking, ramshackle workings of an old rackety machine.

'It's absolutely excruciating!' he exclaimed, throwing his hat down on the bookkeeper's desk. 'It makes you want to prod them like cattle: "Move along there, Daisy! Come on, Buttercup!"'

The bookkeeper, a sickly, jaundiced lad, smiled. He was sprinkling sand onto the large sheet of paper on which he had just been writing and, as he shook the sand off, he said:

'Senhor Machado left a note for you. He said he had to go to Lumiar.'

Mopping his brow with a silk handkerchief, Godofredo gave a faint smile, which he hurriedly concealed beneath his handkerchief. Then he examined the correspondence that the bookkeeper was still sprinkling with sand to dry the ink.

A cart thundered and clanked along the narrow street outside, then all was silence. A clerk was crouched beside an enormous crate in order to write a name on the lid. His quill pen squeaked, and, up above, the clock ticked loudly. In the heat of the day, in the stuffy, low-ceilinged office, there arose from the crates, from two other large bundles and from the dust of the paperwork, a vaguely rancid smell, reminiscent of a grocer's shop.

'I saw Senhor Machado at the theatre last night,' said the bookkeeper, still writing.

Alves, immediately interested, his eyes brighter, put down the letter he was reading:

'Oh, really, what was on?'

'*The Rag-and-Bone Man of Paris*…'

'Any good?'

The bookkeeper looked up from his letter to answer:

'I really liked Teodorico…'

Alves waited for him to say more, to make some critical comment, but the bookkeeper had taken up his quill again, and so he resumed his reading. Then his attention turned for a moment to the clerk crouching by the crate. Alves followed the brushstrokes, enjoying the curves of the letters.

'You've missed off a tilde. Fabião has a tilde on the "a"…'

When the clerk hesitated, he himself crouched down, took the brush and added the missing tilde. He gave a further piece of advice to the bookkeeper about a consignment of red baize being sent to Luanda, then, pushing open another door and going down two steps – the rooms on the mezzanine were on different levels – he went into his office, where he could finally unbutton his waistcoat and flop down in his green-upholstered armchair.

Outside, the July sun blazed down on the stone pavements, but there, in his office, where the sun never penetrated, shaded as it was by the tall buildings opposite, it was always cool; the green shutters were closed, leaving the room in semi-darkness; and the two polished desks – his and that of his partner – the rug on the floor, the spotless green of his chair, the gilt frame surrounding a view of Luanda, the white surround of a large map, all exuded an air of neatness and order, a sense of coolness and repose. There was even a bunch of flowers, sent to him some days earlier by his good wife, Lulu, who felt sorry for him having to spend those hot days in his sweltering office, with no bright flowers to gladden his eye. He had left the flowers on Machado's desk, but without any water the flowers had faded.

The door opened, and the bookkeeper's sallow, sickly face appeared:

'Did Senhor Machado leave any instructions about the Colares wine to be sent to Cabo Verde?'

Then Alves remembered the letter his partner had left on his desk. He opened it. The first few lines explained his reasons for going to Lumiar, but then he got down to business: 'Regarding the Colares wine…' Alves handed the letter to the bookkeeper.

The door closed again, and Alves again smiled as he had before, but making no attempt now to disguise it. This was the fourth or fifth time this month that Machado had absented

himself from the office, saying that he had to go to Lumiar
to see his mother, or cross the river to visit a sick friend, or
else offering no reason at all, merely muttering something
about a 'minor business matter'. Alves knew what that 'minor
business matter' meant. Machado was twenty-six and a
handsome lad, with his fair moustache, curly hair and natural
elegance. Women liked him. Since they had been business
partners, Machado had, to Alves' knowledge, been involved
with three different women: a beautiful Spaniard who had
fallen so passionately in love with him that she had left the rich
Brazilian who had set her up in a house; an actress from the
Teatro Dona Maria, whose sole attraction were her beautiful
eyes; and now this 'minor business matter', which was clearly
a more delicate affair altogether, taking up far more room
in Machado's heart and life. Alves could sense this from his
partner's troubled, anxious look, as if he felt uneasy about
something, even sad. Not that Machado had spoken to him
about it or shown the slightest desire to unburden himself or
confide in him. They were good friends, and Machado often
spent the evening with them at home – where he treated Lulu
almost like a sister – and he had lunch there every Sunday, and
yet – whether because he had joined the firm barely three years
ago, or because he was ten years younger or because Alves
was a friend of his father and one of his father's executors, or
because Alves was married and he was not – Machado always
maintained a vaguely respectful distance, and they had never
enjoyed the kind of camaraderie that usually exists between
men. Alves had, of course, said nothing to Machado about
the 'minor business matter', which had nothing to do with the
company or with him; besides, despite his repeated absences,
Machado continued to be a good worker, always active and
alert and striving to increase the firm's prosperity, and often

spending ten or twelve hours a day glued to his desk when the steamship was in; Alves had to confess that if, in the firm, he himself represented decency, domestic honesty, regularity and propriety, then Machado represented commercial nous, energy, decisiveness, ambition, and business sense. Godofredo had always been lazy by nature, like his father, who, out of choice, used to move from room to room in a wheelchair.

Despite the stern principles and sound beliefs inculcated in him by the Jesuits as a boy, and despite the fact that he had never himself indulged in any pre-marital affairs or unseemly romances, he felt a vague sympathy, a leniency towards Machado's 'youthful follies'. This was, primarily, for reasons of friendship, for he had known Machado ever since he was a cherubic little boy and had always been rather impressed by his chic family, his uncle, the Count de Vilar, his society friendships, by the fuss Dona Maria Forbes made over him, inviting him to her Thursday at-homes – even though he was in commerce – and then there were his refined manners, a certain natural elegance. Alves realised, with some surprise, that he himself could never aspire to such elegance. However, there was another underlying reason for his somewhat reluctant feelings of sympathy for Machado's affairs of the heart; it was a question of temperament really, for, deep down, this thirty-seven-year-old man – already balding, despite his thick black moustache – was a rather fanciful creature. He had inherited this trait from his mother, a thin lady, who played the harp and spent all her time reading poetry. She it was who had given him the ridiculous name of Godofredo. Later on, his mother's sentimentalism, which, for long years, had been channelled into moonlit nights, romantic love and all things literary, became diverted instead towards God, her devotion verging almost on religious mania; that former reader of Lamartine became a maniacal devotee of the Senhor dos Passos – Our Lord of the Stations of the Cross – in Graça; she it was who had chosen a Jesuit education for him – and her final days had been filled with a horror of hell. He had inherited some of those feelings; as a boy, he had been assailed by all kinds of short-lived enthusiasms that shifted back and forth, from the poetry of Almeida Garrett to the Sacred Heart of Jesus. Following a bout of typhoid fever, however, he had calmed down, and when the opportunity came to take over his uncle's import-export business, he became practicality itself, treating life as an entirely material and serious matter; and yet a certain stubborn romanticism lingered in his soul: he loved the theatre, especially melodramas full of violent incident. He read a lot of novels. Grand actions and grand passions excited him. He occasionally felt that he was made for heroism, for tragedy. But these were dim, ill-defined feelings that stirred only rarely in the depths of the heart in which he kept them imprisoned. He was particularly fascinated by romantic passions, not that he himself had ever considered tasting either their honey or their gall; he was a good husband and he loved his wife Lulu, but he did enjoy seeing such passions enacted on the stage or described in books. And he felt intrigued by the romance he sensed was taking place right there in his office; it was as if the faint perfume of romance emanating from Machado made the packages and the paperwork more interesting.

The green baize door opened again, and the bookkeeper's sallow face reappeared. He had come to return Senhor Machado's letter, and, before withdrawing and once more closing the door, he said:

'Tonight is the Annual General Meeting of the Transtagana Company.'

Alves reacted with surprise:

'Is today the ninth, then?'

'It is.'

He knew perfectly well that it was the ninth, but being reminded of that annual general meeting had also reminded him that it was his wedding anniversary. In their first two years of marriage, their anniversary had been the occasion for a small private celebration, with all the family invited to supper, followed by a little dancing to the sound of the piano; their third anniversary had, alas, coincided with the early days of mourning for his mother-in-law, when the house was still sad and Lulu still grieving; and now the date was passing and was, indeed, almost over, with neither of them having given it a thought. He was sure Lulu had forgotten. When he left for work that morning, she had been busy combing her hair and had said nothing, but it would be a shame to let that lovely day pass without them at least drinking a glass of port and enjoying a nice dessert. They should have invited his father-in-law and sister-in-law too, although relations with his father-in-law had cooled slightly of late and a rift opened up, all because of a new young servant girl, who appeared to reign supreme in the widower's house. But on a day like this, as on someone's birthday, such things should be set aside, and family feeling be allowed to prevail. He decided to hurry over to Rua de São Bento, remind Lulu of the important date and send an invitation to his father-in-law, who lived in Rua Santa Isabel. It was nearly three o'clock, he had signed all the correspondence, and there was nothing else that needed doing; it was the calm that always followed the hurly-burly of preparing everything to be sent off on the steam packet to Africa. He picked up his hat, delighting in the half-day holiday he was awarding himself and savouring the idea of surprising his beloved Lulu with an earlier than usual kiss, when, normally, she was left alone until half past four, which was when the office closed. Only one thing bothered him: Machado was in Lumiar and wouldn't be able to join them for supper. The bookkeeper, seeing him with his hat on, asked:

'Will you be coming back, sir?'

For a moment, Godofredo considered inviting the bookkeeper as well, but then feared offending Machado should he learn, later on, that his place at table had been so easily filled.

'No, I won't... If Senhor Machado does come in... he probably won't, but if he does, tell him we expect him at six, as arranged.'

He felt very contented as he went down the steps, as if he had only got married the day before. He was filled with an ardent desire to go home, and, after all that heat, don his linen jacket and his slippers and sit waiting for supper, simply enjoying being there, among the domestic toings and froings, and in the presence of his lovely wife Lulu. Borne along on the wave of happiness that now invaded his soul came the excellent idea of buying Lulu a present. A fan perhaps. No, he would buy her the bracelet he had seen some days before in a jeweller's shopwindow: a ruby-eyed serpent biting its own tail. It was a gift with a meaning, for the serpent symbolised eternity, the certain return of happy days, something revolving for ever in a circle of gold. His only concern was that it might be expensive. In fact, it cost a mere five *libras*, and while he was examining it, the jeweller told him that a few days before, he had sold an identical one to the Marchioness de Lima. Alves bought it on the spot and, shortly after leaving the shop, he paused in the shade, opened the box and looked at the bracelet again, feeling very pleased with his purchase. He felt a rush of tenderness – as often happens when one offers a gift.

It's as if a small door suddenly opens in our natural egotism and greed, allowing in a great swell of latent generosity. At that moment, he wished he were rich enough to give her a diamond necklace, for she certainly deserved it. They had been married for four years, and never a cross word. He had adored her ever since the afternoon in Pedrouços when he first caught sight of her, but – now he could say it – he had also felt rather afraid of her. She had seemed to him so imperious, so proud, demanding and brusque. That, however, was simply the impression caused by her height, her fine dark eyes, her erect carriage, her thick, wavy hair. Inside that tyrannical, queenly body beat the heart of a child. She was kind, charitable, merry, and her temperament was as calm and placid as the transparent surface of a river in summer. For a while, about four months ago, she had grown moody, somewhat melancholy and nervy; indeed, he had even thought… but no, that, alas, had not been the reason. Her nerves were on edge, that was all, and the mood had passed quickly enough; indeed, lately, she had never been more loving, more cheerful, more capable of filling him with joy…

These thoughts continued to dance gaily about in his heart as he walked up Rua Nova do Carmo, shading himself from the baking heat with his parasol. At the top of the street, he called in at Restaurante Mata to order a fish pie for six o'clock. He also bought some ham and looked around for other possible purchases, with all the eager joy of a bird providing for its nestlings.

Then he walked up the Chiado, where he paused to gaze respectfully at a great man, a real character, a poet and historian, who happened to be standing chatting to someone at the door of Bertrand's Bookshop; he was wearing an old lustrine jacket and a straw hat and was about to blow his nose on a vast flowered handkerchief. Godofredo admired both the man's novels and his style. Then he bought some cigars, not for himself, because he didn't smoke, but to give to his father-in-law after supper. Then, finally, he proceeded down Calçada do Correio, which lay glittering, dry and dusty in the sun. He walked briskly, despite the heat, occasionally touching the box containing the bracelet, which he had put in his frock-coat pocket.

He was in Rua de São Bento, just a few steps from his house, when he spotted his maid, Margarida, waiting at the counter in the cake shop. Lulu had not, after all, forgotten that happy date, for Margarida had clearly been sent out to buy cakes for dessert. He went in through the street door. They lived in a two-storey house, squeezed in between two other larger buildings, and painted blue: they occupied the first floor, and although he disliked his upstairs neighbours – noisy, vulgar people – and would have preferred not to share with them the little touches of luxury he gave to his hallway, he had, at Lulu's request, paid to have the stairs carpeted. And he was glad now that he had, because it was always a pleasure, whenever he went into the house, to feel the carpet beneath his feet and see it rolling away up the stairs, giving the place a sense of solid comfort. It somehow boosted his self-esteem. Upstairs, Margarida, who would doubtless be back shortly, had left the door to their apartment open, and inside there reigned a great silence; in the intense afternoon heat, everything seemed to be sleeping. Brilliant sun flooded in through the skylight; the bell pull, with its large scarlet ball on one end, hung motionless.

Then he had the absurd idea, worthy of a playful newlywed, of tiptoeing into the bedroom and surprising Lulu, who, at that hour, would normally be getting dressed for dinner. And he smiled to think of the little shriek she would utter as she

sat there, perhaps still in her white petticoat, her lovely arms
bare. He went, first, into the dining room, which led through
two curtained doorways into her boudoir and the parlour. His
thin-soled summer shoes made no noise on the carpets. The
whole apartment seemed uninhabited and so silent that one
could hear the sound of frying coming from the kitchen and
the canary hopping about inside its cage on the balcony. The
curtain covering the door to her room was drawn shut, and
he, still wearing the same gentle smile, was just about to draw
it back and startle her when he heard through the half-drawn
curtain covering the door opposite, the door into the parlour,
a faint sound, vague and indistinct, like a throaty sigh. He
turned when he realised that she was in there and peered round
the curtain. And what he saw, dear God, made him freeze,
stopped his breath, sent his blood rushing to his head, and so
pierced his heart that he almost fainted... Sitting on the yellow
damask sofa, next to a low table on which stood a bottle of
wine, was Lulu in her white peignoir; and she was leaning
in an abandoned fashion against the shoulder of a man, who
had his waistcoat unbuttoned and his arm about her waist and
was gazing down at her with soft, languid eyes. That man was
Machado.

II

When the curtain twitched aside, Ludovina saw Godofredo,
screamed, and instinctively jumped up and away from the sofa.
Godofredo heard that scream, but couldn't move, somehow
he found himself sitting on a chair by the door, trembling as
furiously as if he had a fever. Through the febrile fog filling
his head and emptying it of ideas, he could hear the confusion

in the room. Heavy footsteps on the carpet, a few anxious, whispered words, then the bolt on the door leading to the stairs being drawn back, and after that, silence. However, his strength quickly returned, along with the thought that they had both fled; gripped by fury, he hurled himself into the room, where he stumbled on a fox-fur stole lying across the threshold and fell, ridiculously, face forwards onto the rug. When he struggled to his feet again, fists clenched, the curtain covering the door to the stairs was swaying in the breeze and there was no one in the room. He ran to the landing, where, before him, beneath the glare from the skylight, lay the deserted stairs, with their smug air of decency. He rushed like a madman to the window, where he saw Machado, parasol in hand, striding rapidly away down the street. But where was she? When he turned, a terrified Margarida was standing in the middle of the room, clutching her box of cakes.

'Where is she?' bawled Godofredo.

Margarida didn't immediately understand what he meant, but then, suddenly, she dropped the box of cakes on the floor, raised her apron to her face and burst into tears. He pushed her aside, almost hurling her to the floor, and ran into the kitchen. The cook had the door closed and was singing loudly for the benefit of the courtyard while she scaled the fish, and so had heard nothing, knew nothing. Then Godofredo flung himself at the door of Ludovina's bedroom. It was locked.

'Open up or I'll break the door down!'

There was no reply: he pressed his ear to the wood; from within came a muffled sobbing, a mixture of anxiety and fear.

'Open up or I'll break it down,' he shouted again, hammering on the door, as if he were already beating her body, his mind filled with ideas of blood and death.

Then a frightened, pleading voice came from within:

'Promise you won't hurt me.'

'I promise, but open this door!'

The key turned in the lock. He rushed in, while Ludovina, in her long white peignoir, took refuge behind the bed, clasping her hands, her tear-filled eyes wide with terror.

Confronted by this weeping woman, his throat tightened, and he could find not a single word to say; he merely fixed her with a mad stare, almost in tears himself.

She took two steps towards him, her arms wide, her voice trembling, the whole of her trembling, then cried out tearfully:

'Oh, Godofredo, forgive me, please, I didn't do anything wrong, it was the first time...'

And he, his throat still tight, could only manage to say through gritted teeth:

'The first time, the first time...'

His rage rose inside him and exploded in a scream:

'What do you mean "the first time", there should never have been a first time, you hussy! And with him of all people. I should kill you right now. But go, get out of here, leave me, woman. Go on, go!'

She left the room, sobbing desperately. Then, turning, he saw the cook standing in the doorway, watching, eyes ablaze with curiosity, and out in the corridor, in the shadows, stood the hunched, frightened, inquisitive figure of Margarida.

'What are you doing here?' he yelled. 'Get back to the kitchen this minute! And if one word of this gets out, you're fired!'

With that, he slammed the door and started pacing furiously up and down, where the large bed glowed, ostentatious in its whiteness, its two pillows lying close together. Through the blood boiling in his head, his ideas began slowly to come into focus; he decided that he would fight a duel to the death with

Machado and pack Lulu off to her father's house. He briefly considered sending her to a convent, but it seemed more dignified simply to return her to her father. And as soon as he had gauged, weighed and fixed on these two resolutions, his rage subsided.

Now there was just a hard, black sadness in which was mingled the cold, sharp, imperative need for revenge. The house seemed once again to be sleeping in the sun, preserving only a faint remnant of the anger it had witnessed.

He tried then to compose his face; he even stood in front of the mirror and straightened his tie, before pushing open the door to the dining room. There she was, sitting on a chair, leaning against the wall, her handkerchief in her hand, quietly weeping and occasionally blowing her nose. Her lovely hair was still caught up in a scarlet net, and her peignoir had come undone to reveal the lace trim on her nightdress and part of one white breast. He averted his eyes, not even wanting to see her weeping. Still turned to the window, he said harshly, abruptly:

'Get your things together, you're off to your father's house.'

Still looking out of the window, he sensed that the soft weeping behind him had stopped, but she did not respond. He waited for a word of repentance, for her to plead with him in the name of their friendship. He heard only the sound of her blowing her nose. Then he waxed cruel. In a spectral voice uttered by a mouth of stone, he spoke words intended to burn:

'I don't want prostitutes living in my house. You can take everything, everything that belongs to you. But I want you out of here!'

He turned and went straight to his study, a small room containing only a writing desk and a bookcase. He sat down, took a sheet of paper and wrote the date at the top in a tremulous hand that distorted his usually fine italic script. Then

he hesitated; should he put: 'Dear Papa' or 'Sir'? He opted for
the latter given that they were no longer related, given that
he no longer had any family. And faced by the blank piece
of paper, he pondered that thought – he no longer had any
family. He was filled with self-pity. Why was this happening
to him, he who had always been so hard-working, so good, he
who had loved her so much? His eyes filled with tears. But he
didn't want to get upset, he wanted to write his letter – coldly,
stiffly. However, when he took out his handkerchief, he found
a box, the box containing the bracelet. He opened it and sat
looking at the bracelet for a moment; in its nest of silk lay the
golden serpent with the ruby eyes, still biting its own tail, that
beautiful symbol of eternity, the certain return of happy days,
over and over, for ever and ever. He felt a furious urge to crush
Ludovina, to throw in her face all his kindnesses to her, his
sacrifices, the dresses he had bought for her, the whims he had
granted, the boxes at the theatre, his dedication and his love.
Unable to contain himself, he marched back into the dining
room, his lips full of rebuke. She was still there, standing up
now, wiping her eyes, and staring stupidly out at the building
opposite, just as he had before. Her lovely profile was bathed
in light, her petticoat clung to the soft, strong, graceful curves
of her body. And suddenly Godofredo felt all those words of
rebuke dry up in his mouth. He could find no way of launching
into that stream of invective; he stood at the other window,
angrily twirling his moustache, his heart in turmoil, his lips
dumb. At last, an absurd idea rose up from his romantic depths.
He flung the bracelet down on the table and shouted:

'You can put that in your suitcase too. I bought it for you
today. Yet another present!'

Instinctively, she glanced at the box, then started crying
again.

Those mute tears bothered and irritated him.

'Why all the tears? Whose fault is this, eh? It's certainly not mine, because you've certainly never lacked for anything…'

And then came the explosion. Striding up and down the room, speaking very quickly and quietly, he threw in her face all his love, all his devotion. She, meanwhile, had collapsed into a chair, still crying. It seemed as if she would cry for ever. He bawled:

'Stop crying will you and speak! Explain yourself! Have you nothing to say on your behalf? Were you the one who wanted it, the one who started it?'

From where she sat she looked sharply up at him. And through the tears, a light came into her eyes. Breathlessly, like someone clinging on to something in order not to fall, she laid all the blame on Machado. It had been entirely his fault. It had begun four months ago, when he had finished with that actress from the Teatro Dona Maria. He had suddenly turned his attentions on her, talking to her, tempting her, writing to her and visiting her when Godofredo was at the office; then one day, almost by force…

'I swear that's how it was… I didn't want to, I begged him…Then I was afraid Margarida might hear the noise…'

Godofredo listened, ashen-faced.

'Let me see his letters,' he said at last, in a barely audible voice.

'I haven't got them.'

He took a step towards her bedroom, saying:

'I'll find them.'

She sprang to her feet with a cry, folding him in her arms:

'I swear I don't have them. As God is my witness. I returned them all to him days ago…'

He pushed her away and went over to the dressing table. A

28

bunch of keys lay on the marble top, along with various bottles. And then began a desperate search among the handkerchiefs and the lace, in the boxes of fans and other such intimate feminine accoutrements.

She occasionally seized his arm and again swore that there were no letters. Again, he gently pushed her away and continued to wreak havoc in the drawers. An ivory fan fell and broke; a rosary with its cross lay on the floor.

And just when it seemed that she was telling him the truth, suddenly, right before his eyes, between two hairbrushes, he saw the bundle of letters, tied with a silk ribbon. He grabbed the bundle and untied it; they were not Machado's letters, but hers. He opened the first, which began, 'My angel'. Then he calmly stuffed them into his pocket, turned to her, where she lay prostrate on the edge of the bed, and said:

'Get yourself ready to leave the house today.'

He returned to his study, where he read each letter. They could not have been more imbecilic, the endless repetition of the same old clichés: 'My adored angel, why did God not let us meet long ago?...'My love, are you thinking of the one who would give her life for you?' And even: 'Ah, how I wish I could have your child…'

Each sentence fell upon his heart like a dull, devastating blow. Then, almost tearing the paper with the quill, he scrawled a letter to his father-in-law, just a few simple words explaining that he had found his wife with another man and wanted him, the father-in-law, to come and fetch her. If he did not, he would put her out in the street, like a whore, with no regard to her fate. A postscript added that he would be away from the house between five and seven that evening, and asked that his father-in-law take advantage of that absence to collect his daughter.

Then he put the letter in his pocket, buttoned up his frock

coat, briefly buffed the silk of his hat with his sleeve, and left. On the stairs, he met a boy wearing a white apron and carrying a basket.

'Is this where Senhor Alves lives?'

It was the fish pie, the ham, the cheese, and all the other good things he had bought. Sadness filled his heart. He had to grab hold of the banister so as not to faint; the boy stared at him in alarm. Alves asked:

'Are you from the restaurant?'

'Yes, sir,' answered the boy, still alarmed by the sight of this apparently ill man.

Godofredo murmured:

'Go upstairs and knock on the door.'

He stayed on the stairs, listening. He heard the boy's knocking, heard the door open, and then Margarida's voice saying to her mistress inside:

'It's a boy with a pie, Senhora.'

He took the remaining stairs four at a time, then, once at the bottom, and as if under the influence of the staircase's grave air of decency, he tried to calm himself, buttoned up his frock coat, ran his hands over his face, and prepared to walk past his neighbours with his customary aplomb, thus assuring him of their continued esteem and respect.

III

Fortunately, a man who sometimes ran errands for him – often to his father-in-law's house – was standing outside the grocer's opposite. Godofredo gave him the letter, telling him to hand it to the addressee himself and not to wait for a reply.

And despite knowing the man's probity, for he had grown old in the job, he added:

'Mind now, give it to the addressee himself, there's money inside, a bank note.'

The old man placed the letter next to his heart, under his shirt.

And Godofredo followed him and the letter from afar.

He watched as the man went into the father-in-law's house, a grubby, four-storey building, with a junk shop at street level. Neto lived on the top floor, the one with a flowerpot on the balcony. And for what seemed like an eternity, Alves stood watching the door from a distance. The messenger did not reappear. Godofredo was gripped by a terrible thought: What if his father-in-law wasn't at home? What if he only returned after dark, what if he had dined out and would not be back until nightfall? What was he to do? Roam the streets, waiting for his wife to leave? This thought filled him with a sense of desolation and disorder, as if all regularity were at an end. Then he saw the messenger. He had, as per instructions, delivered the letter to Senhor Neto himself and left at once, without waiting for an answer. Much relieved, Godofredo continued walking, going nowhere in particular, but his steps instinctively carried him along the route he followed each morning, to his office. He walked down the Chiado. In Rua do Ouro, he paused for a moment to look at a pistol in Lebreton's shop window. And the thought of death pierced him. But he didn't want to think about that, not now, nor about the duel. Only when he went back home at seven o'clock and found the house empty would he think about the duel, about settling accounts with that other man. And he continued his random wanderings. For a moment, he considered going to the Passeio Público, but feared bumping into Machado there. He walked instead across Terreiro do

Paço, down the Aterro, almost as far as Rua da Alcântara. He was moving like a sleepwalker, not even noticing the jostling crowd or the lovely summer evening, which was dying now in a splendid glow of bright gold. He wasn't thinking about anything in particular: ideas flowed through him, all kinds of things passed through his head, memories of his courting days with Ludovina, the outings they had enjoyed together, the way she had been leaning against that other man, with the bottle of port wine before them; and again and again he recalled fragments of those letters: 'My angel, how I wish I could have your child.' This was precisely what she used to say to him, her lips on his lips, at night in their warm bed. He was glad now that he had never had a child with the shameless hussy.

As it grew dark, he considered going home. After all the emotions of the day, after the long walk in the soft July air, he felt suddenly profoundly tired. He went into a café and drank a large glass of water, then sat, leaning his head against the wall, surrendering to that brief respite. The bar lay in semi-darkness. A warm dusk enfolded the city; all the windows were open, breathing in the air after the great heat of the day; the occasional light came on, and people walked by, hat in hand. And he took pleasure in that restful gloom, as if, in that state of inertia, among the shadows of the coming night, his pain were dissipating, dissolving. He wished he could stay there for ever, that the lamps would remain unlit, that he would never need to take another step. And the idea of death assailed him, serene and insinuating, like the merest breath of a caress. He really did want to die. His body felt so exhausted that all the bitterness still to come, the cruel thoughts, the empty house, the encounter with Machado, the need to find seconds, all seemed such burdensome tasks, as unbearably heavy as rocks that his poor hands would never be able to lift. How delicious it would be to stay there on that bench, dead, free, beyond all pain, having departed life as silently and tranquilly as the dying light. For a moment, he considered suicide. It didn't terrify him, he didn't even quail before the idea of killing himself, but finding a weapon or throwing himself into the river required effort, and in his current will-less state, he found any effort repellent. He wanted to die right there, without having to move. If all it took was a word, a quiet order telling his heart to stop and grow cold, he would quite happily say that word. And she perhaps would weep for him and miss him. But the other man?

The thought of 'the other man' restored to him a certain degree of resolve and at least enough energy to get up and continue his walk. Yes, if he were simply to disappear that night, the other man would be very pleased indeed. It would be a source of enormous relief to him. He would feign grief for a few days, he might even feel genuinely upset, but then he would simply get on with his life; the firm would become Machado & Co.; he would continue to have his mistresses, go to the theatre, and wax his moustache. And that was most unfair. After all, it was he who had brought about the ruin of another man's happiness, and he was the one who deserved to die. Yes, it was Machado who should disappear; he was the one who should kill himself. That would be real justice. And then everything would work out quite differently: the firm would continue to be called Alves & Co., and, later on, Godofredo could become reconciled with his wife, and life would continue calmly and resignedly. That was how it should be. If God were to look first at one and then at the other, weighing up the merits and faults of each man, He would surely make Machado disappear and inspire *him* with thoughts of suicide.

And then, out of these two absurd imaginings that came and

went in his troubled mind – his suicide and that of the other man – an idea surfaced, like a bright lightning flash among dark clouds, an idea clear in every detail, which seemed to him both fair and feasible, the most convenient course of action and the only dignified one.

Just at that moment, however, something familiar about the houses he was passing made him realise that he was actually outside his own front door. He stopped, overwhelmed by thoughts of Ludovina, and stared at the house. With the gaslight outside, with its immaculate, blue-painted façade and its green shutters, it stood, between the two tall buildings on either side, like a symbol of decency. No lights were on in their apartment, and the street door was closed. Would she still be there? Had her father come to fetch her? A terrible anxiety set his heart pounding. For a second, he wished she was still there and even considered forgiving her, so frightening did he find that empty house. Then he decided that, from now on, he would treat her coldly, stiffly; no, best never to see her again. Curiosity took him to his father-in-law's house at the other end of the street, to that tall, neglected, grubby building. The windows on the third floor stood open to the cool of the night, but no lights were on there either. Neither of those two façades spoke to him or eased his disquiet.

He returned home and pushed open the street door. The carpeted stairs slept in the warm glow of the gaslight, and the muffled sound of his footsteps seemed to him to echo in a hollow, empty space. From the second floor came the vaguely religious sound of a piano, playing something from *Faust*. The people above were happy.

The cook came to open the door to him, and something in her manner told Godofredo at once that Ludovina had left.

In the dining room, a candle had been placed on the table

cloth. He picked it up and went into his bedroom, where he saw two suitcases and a trunk. However, some of her possessions were still there: next to the bed stood her slippers and on the chaise longue lay the white peignoir she had been wearing that morning. Other things, though, had already been packed away: the glass bottles on the dressing table, a wooden Virgin of which she was particularly fond. He put the candle down on the dressing table, and his face appeared to him in the mirror, pale, suddenly older, staring back at him with a ruined, abandoned air.

He picked up the candle again and went into the parlour, in which catastrophe still seemed to linger. The fox fur stole was still there on the floor; on the table next to the sofa stood the bottle of port, and on the table edge, was the other man's stubbed-out cigar. Faced by that cigar stub, he was filled by a wave of silent rage; he felt as if he had been slapped across the face by an iron hand; he trembled under the impact of a gross insult, and swore to harden himself, never to forgive, even to despatch her remaining luggage himself – and to see that other man dead at his feet or to die himself.

This, however, was followed by an immediate resolve to resist that troubled, disquieting state. He wanted to restore order to his mind, and for the house to recover its air of ordinary calm. She had left, and her luggage would follow that very night. Thenceforth, he would be a widower, but the household would continue to function in a serene and orderly fashion.

He called for Margarida.

'Is there no supper to be had in this house tonight? Why is the table not set?'

The maid stared at him, as if astonished that he should want to dine, still less in that house. She was clearly about to say something, but he gave her such a determined look that she scuttled from the room and, moments later, was hurriedly, zealously setting the table as if anxious to be forgiven for any apparent complicity with her mistress. She placed on the table everything that had been delivered in the basket – the pie, the ham, the fruit tart.

Godofredo, meanwhile, had gone to his study. The idea that had flashed through his mind when he returned from his walk, and which now seemed to him the only possible solution, returned and took root in his mind, becoming the centre of all his thoughts. It was this: he and the other man should draw lots to decide who should kill himself!

This idea seemed to him neither excessive nor tragic nor disproportionate; on the contrary, it was perfectly rational and dignified, and, more than that, the only possible choice. He felt that he was reasoning with absolute clarity. A duel with swords, two businessmen in shirtsleeves making clumsy, pointless stabs at each other, until one of them received a wound to the arm – that seemed ridiculous, as ridiculous as an exchange of bullets; they would doubtless both miss, then get into their respective hired carriages along with their seconds and go their separate ways. No, death was the only proper punishment for such an insult: two pistols, only one of which was loaded, to be chosen at random and then fired at point-blank range. But that was impossible. Where would they find seconds willing to share responsibility for such a tragedy? There would be no point trying to explain the situation to them: adultery is a grave thing for the husband, but for others it was merely a misfortune, a failure, but not one that calls for bloody revenge. Besides, if he were to die, that would be an end to the matter, but if he saw the other man fall dead at his feet, what would his life be like after that? He would have to flee, abandon his business, and seek his fortune in a foreign land. But where? And the difficulty remained: they would never find seconds to agree to such a 'duel'. Then there would be the scandal, the gossip, the truth that would, inevitably, come out. This other possibility, though, was easy, secret, decent and would involve no one else. They would draw lots, and the loser would agree to kill himself within a year. If he lost, he wouldn't hesitate, he would kill himself at once. And he didn't doubt for a moment that Machado would agree to this! How could he refuse? He had dishonoured him and must pay with his blood. At the same time, he had a vague presentiment that he would be the one to lose… And then that would be that – so much the better. What pleasure could life bring him now, alone for ever in that house, robbed of any satisfaction he took in his work? Because he got no satisfaction from spending the money he earned. He hesitated not a moment longer; he wrote a short note to Machado, asking him to meet him the following day, Sunday, at eleven o'clock in the morning, in the office. He was just sealing the letter when Margarida arrived to tell him that supper was served. He quickly put on his hat, went out into the street, posted the letter in the box next to the grocer's and returned to the dining room, where both the cook and Margarida were standing next to the rapidly cooling tureen of soup, astonished at their master's behaviour. Margarida's presence there made him feel uncomfortable; he sensed that she had been an accomplice and had known about the infamous affair. He briefly considered sacking her on the spot, but that would be like giving the maid's tongue free rein in other households, in the houses of tattletales, where she could tell everyone about his misfortune. He decided not to get rid of her and to put up with her presence, while keeping her in constant fear of dismissal and thus ensuring her silence.

He had just unfolded his napkin and lifted the lid of the soup tureen, when the doorbell rang loudly.

Margarida went to answer, and his heart beat furiously. The girl came running back and declared, as if she were announcing the arrival of Providence itself, come to punish and restore:

'Sir, it's Senhor Neto!'

IV

Neto entered the room. When he saw the table laid, saw the large pie and the ham, saw Godofredo with his napkin tucked into his collar and a bottle of wine beside him, he stood in the doorway, somewhat taken aback, clutching his hat in one hand and his cane in the other. Finally, he muttered somewhat bitterly:

'I see you haven't lost your appetite.'

Godofredo immediately sprang to his feet, took a candle from the sideboard and was about to go into the parlour, but Neto said:

'No, please, there's plenty of time to talk, finish your supper first.'

After raising one spoonful of soup to his mouth, however, Alves pushed away the plate and rang the bell. Neto, meanwhile, was slowly setting down his hat and cane on a chair, filling the silence with his languid movements. He was a large, well-built man, who had been handsome in his day, and he still had a strong profile, to which his extremely pale skin lent elegance and distinction. He wore two strands of hair meticulously combed over his bald head, and his moustache looked as if it had been cut absolutely straight with one snip of the scissors; his slightest gesture oozed dignity and seriousness, so that even now, as he removed his gloves, he appeared to be performing some important official function.

The maid had brought in the stew and was lingering at the table in the hope of overhearing something. Adopting the air of a society man, Neto remained studiously indifferent and nonchalant, saying only that it was hellishly hot.

'Indeed,' said Godofredo, who had not raised his eyes from the table since Neto had entered the room but sat in his chair, twiddling one end of his moustache and keeping his other hand in his pocket. At last, the maid left, with orders not to return until he rang again. He then got up and shut the door after her.

Seeing that he could now speak freely, Neto perched on the edge of a chair, rubbed his knees for a moment, and said in a slow, studied voice, intended to be eloquent and impressive:

'I have done my duty as a father...'

For a moment, he watched his son-in-law, expecting some interruption, a word at least. However, Godofredo was helping himself to some rice. Neto went on:

'Yes, I have done my duty as a father, and am still doing so now as we speak. As soon as I received your letter, as soon as I saw that there had been some domestic upset, I came to fetch my daughter, to allow time for explanations, to give you both a chance to clear up any misunderstanding. When two people fall out, it is always best for them to go their separate ways for a time. Such matters are best dealt with calmly and at a distance. If you stay cooped up together, it's all too easy to let your tongue run away with you, and then it's downhill all the way.'

He was rapidly running out of solemn words and, in his excitement, clumsier, more vulgar expressions were finding their way into his speech.

'Anyway,' he concluded, 'all I want to know is what all the fuss is about.'

Godofredo had listened in silence, picking indifferently at a few grains of rice. He was determined not to get angry, to be respectful but firm. He despised his father-in-law because of certain distasteful rumours he had heard about him, notably regarding his grubby affair with his maid. He was not impressed by his solemn air and brought him to heel with a few brief, well-chosen words.

'The "fuss", as you call it, is precisely as I explained in my letter. I found your daughter with another man and sent her home to you.'

Neto shuddered. Alves' brusque tone was like an insult flung in his face. He stood up, eyes blazing, his bald head scarlet:

'Really! And what if I don't want her at home with me? It's simply not on, you know. You can't just marry a girl, keep her for four years and then, at the end of the four years, send her back to her father! It's simply not on! What if I don't want her at home with me, what then?'

He was waving his arms about, all diplomacy forgotten, in a voice that could have been heard in the kitchen.

Godofredo said very coolly:

'Then put her out in the street.'

This was too much for Neto.

'In the street? In the street!'

'Of course. She dishonoured me, dishonoured my house, and I won't allow that. So she can pack her bags and be off! If her father doesn't want her, if nobody wants her, then obviously, she'll have to stay out in the street.'

Neto could not believe such implacable stubbornness. He had folded his arms and was staring at his son-in-law, eyes

40

aflame.

'Let me take a good look at you, just to make sure that you are not a monster. You're saying that you would abandon your wife and leave her out in the street, with no shelter?'

These words were torture to Godofredo. It was like poking around in a still bleeding wound. He stood up, intending to say something to bring the discussion to a close, but Neto would not allow him to speak. He bawled:

'Besides, you don't throw a woman out of her house just because she was alone with a visitor!'

Godofredo stood staring at his father-in-law, lips trembling, unable to utter the words choking him. It horrified him having to say out loud, even to his father-in-law, how he had found her in the arms of another man. In the face of this silence, Neto waxed triumphant:

'You have to prove it! The law requires her to have been found *in flagrante*. You saw nothing, you've never even read a single letter...'

At this point, Godofredo's rage exploded:

'The letters, sir, were unspeakable! Obscene! Do you know what she wrote to him? She said she wanted his child! A child that I would then have to clothe, feed, love and bring up. A child! Is that how you brought up your daughter to behave?'

Neto sat with head bowed. His daughter had not told him about the letters. Looking bewildered, he smoothed the two strands of hair covering his bald pate, then, after a long silence, murmured:

'When a woman gets a mad idea in her head, she'll write all kinds of nonsense.'

Godofredo did not respond. He was pacing up and down the room, his hands in his pockets, and on the table, his plate of rice stood forgotten and rapidly cooling. Neto downed a large glass of water. Then, as if he had finally screwed up the necessary courage, he blurted out the real matter that had brought him there.

'But what do you expect her to live on? I don't have enough money to keep her in clothes or even shoes!'

Godofredo immediately stopped his gloomy pacing. He had been expecting this, he was prepared and had his answer ready; in the dignified tone of a man who was above such footling matters as money, he said:

'As long as your daughter remains in your house and behaves herself, she will receive thirty *mil réis* a month.'

Neto's bald head seemed to light up; he appeared suddenly completely satisfied, all anger gone.

'That's very reasonable,' he said, almost touched, 'very reasonable indeed.'

Then the two men fell silent, as if there were nothing more to be said.

Godofredo rang the bell, and the maid came running in, her eyes darting from one man to the other.

'Serve the coffee,' said Alves.

'And a cup for me too, Senhora Margarida,' said Neto, falling back into his familiar ways as father-in-law of the household.

Godofredo continued his pacing, while Neto sat down at the table and carefully rolled a cigarette, shooting an occasional sideways glance at his son-in-law. It seemed to take him an eternity to prepare a satisfactorily smooth, plump cigarette, put his tobacco pouch back in his pocket, and take out a match. Finally, he gave a kind of sigh and said:

'Of course, the worst thing is the gossip!'

Godofredo said nothing while Neto slowly lit his cigarette.

'And it can only do harm to a man in your position, a

42

businessman…'

Godofredo spun round impatiently:

'And whose fault is that?'

No, no, it wasn't his fault at all. Neto knew that perfectly well, but, it would, nonetheless, be best to avoid gossip, at least in the early days.

Margarida returned with the coffee. Godofredo had sat down. Father-in-law and son-in-law sat face to face for a moment, stirring in their sugar. Neto tasted his coffee and added still more sugar. Then he took two puffs on his cigarette before returning to his theme:

'No, it won't do either of us any good if people start to talk.'

Neto's slowness and his painful pauses were beginning to irritate Godofredo.

'What is it exactly that you want me to do?'

Neto maintained his calm, reflective air, and expressed his feelings in an equally serene voice. He had, he said, always thought of himself as a good father, and in different circumstances, he would never dream of accepting an allowance for his daughter or, indeed, of asking for anything else. He would simply take her home, where they would all live together, and that would be that. He would also do all he could to silence any scandal.

Godofredo was beginning to understand. Neto had another idea for getting money out of him, and Godofredo wanted to know what it was.

'Enough beating about the bush, sir, what precisely do you have in mind?'

Neto, however, continued his beating. The best way to avoid scandal would be to leave Lisbon. And it was the right season for it too, the ideal time for a little sea-bathing; no one would be surprised, for example, if he went off to Ericeira taking his married daughter with him. Everyone would assume that Alves was too busy to accompany her, and there would be no way of knowing whether or not he visited his wife every week or not. As an idea, it was perfect, but...

Godofredo interrupted him:

'But you want me to give you the money for it.'

'Well, I wouldn't want to rob you,' said Neto with unusual frankness.

Godofredo considered this request. It was clearly a clever way of getting to spend the summer at the beach – at his expense; but it was also very sensible and would certainly put paid to the gossip. He agreed, and they quickly sorted out the details. Godofredo would pay thirty *libras* to cover the cost of renting a house in Ericeira and the transportation of any furniture, as well as providing a daily allowance; in the months of August, September and October, moreover, Ludovina's monthly allowance would be increased to fifty *mil réis*, to take account of any minor expenditures at the beach. As soon as he had said this, Godofredo got up, wanting to end the interview there and then.

'And now let's speak no more of the matter. My head is spinning.'

He did, indeed, look terribly pale and could feel a headache coming on, along with a great desire to lie down and sleep for a very long time.

Neto, however, wanted to have the last word. From now on, he declared, he would be entirely responsible for his daughter. He put his trust in God, however, and was sure that in time, when the initial pain had passed, they would reach an understanding and be reconciled.

Godofredo shook his head, smiling sadly. No, there could

be no reconciliation.

'The future belongs to God,' said Neto. 'Now, I agree absolutely that it's best for you to separate for a while, and that is what I was coming to. For as long as she is living in my house, it will be as if she were in a convent. I will answer for her every move.'

Godofredo gave a slight shrug. Everything his father-in-law said seemed to him mere empty words. What he wanted now was to be alone. He had rung the bell, and Margarida was ready to open the front door and light Senhor Neto on his way. Neto picked up his hat and, still standing, took a last sip of coffee; then, after shaking his son-in-law's hand, he left, murmuring to the maid that she should have her mistress's luggage ready and waiting.

'Oh, and she asked you not to forget the little silver sugar bowl that was a birthday gift from her godfather. It does, after all, belong to her.'

With that, he went down the stairs, feeling very pleased with himself. His daughter had, in fact, said nothing to him about the sugar bowl. But it was hers, and a very nice piece of silverware, and it was only right that it should return home with her.

It was a humid night, and Neto walked slowly back to his house, carrying his hat in his hand, calculating how much their stay in Ericeira would cost. A little sea-bathing would do him good too. He could live in some comfort on Ludovina's monthly allowance of fifty *mil réis*, and, given that it was probably best that Ludovina appeared in public as little as possible, she wouldn't need any new dresses, and he could even pocket some of the money himself.

When he had toiled up the one hundred and fifty stairs to their apartment, he rang the bell, and Teresa, his unmarried daughter, rushed excitedly to open the door, her eyes shining. No one had concealed the truth from her. She knew that Ludovina had been caught with a man, that there had been a terrible scene, and that her father had gone to talk to Godofredo.

'So what happened?' she asked eagerly.

'We'll talk inside.'

They crossed the kitchen, which lay in darkness, apart from the glow from the coals in the stove, on top of which the kettle was boiling, and went into the dining room, a cramped space at the back of the house. At a round table sat the maid, Senhora Joana, a robust young woman, wearing a dress of blue merino wool and a pair of earrings fine enough for a lady. While she read the newspaper by the light of an oil-lamp, a silent Ludovina, entirely dressed in black, sat slumped in a wicker chair in the darkness by the sideboard.

When her father came in, she sat up, her eyes still red.

Neto sat down, mopping the sweat from his brow with his silk handkerchief. The three women were almost devouring him with their eyes. And when he continued to take his time, savouring the general anxiety, it was Senhora Joana who finally cried:

'Come on then, speak!'

He slowly put away his handkerchief and, in the deep silence of the room, announced:

'Godofredo is willing to pay thirty *mil réis* a month.'

There was a quiet sigh of relief, a tremor of satisfaction. Teresa was staring open-mouthed at Ludovina, astonished to learn that such a large amount of money should fall into her sister's pocket after she had been caught *in flagrante* with another man. Senhora Joana thought it a very gentlemanly gesture. Only Ludovina saw nothing extraordinary about it: after all, he could hardly kick her out of the house without a penny.

Then her father turned to her, frowning.

'You told me that there had been no correspondence. He says he found some indecent letters in your bedroom.'

'It's a lie,' she said simply, 'there was nothing in the letters. It was all a joke.'

A silence fell, while Neto, looking down at the table top, smoothed the strands of hair over his bald pate. The three women continued to stare at him, eager for more details of the interview.

'And what about Lulu's suitcases, Papa?' asked Teresa, who had spent the whole afternoon waiting for the cases to arrive, hoping to see them unpacked and perhaps get a present for herself.

Her Papa, however, had his mind on other things and, without answering her, continued:

'And it's been agreed that, to avoid gossip, we will all go and spend the summer in Ericeira.'

This announcement was greeted with joy by both Teresa, who clapped her hands, and by Joana, who laughed contentedly, because she was much in need of some sea-bathing. Only Ludovina remained indifferent, a shadow of sadness on her face, thinking, rather, of the delightful plan Godofredo had been hatching lately, of spending August and September in Sintra. And she resumed her sitting, while Joana and Teresa pestered their father with questions, both of them already full of plans and thrilled at the prospect of spending the summer by the sea. They positively overflowed with ideas. Teresa prattled away, and Joana kept thinking of all the things they would have to take with them: mattresses, crockery, and, if they were really to enjoy themselves, the piano. The best of it was that they would all be going to Ericeira together and renting a house. Then Ludovina emerged from her silence:

'We need a house we can all fit into… I don't want to have to sleep in a pokey little room like this.'

Her father frowned at such exigencies and retorted:

'You'll sleep where you can. If you want to live in a nice big house like your husband's, then you should have behaved yourself.'

Another silence fell. No one ever dared answer back when Neto raised his voice. Then, in the midst of the frightened, respectful silence carved out by his anger, he took a pencil from his pocket, put his glasses on his nose and, by the light of the oil-lamp, began to calculate, in the margin of the newspaper, what their expenses in Ericeira would be. Leaning across the table, Teresa watched the column of numbers growing – so much for the house, so much for the carriage to take them there – as if the numbers were a string of glittering pleasures. Behind her stood Joana, who added her own suggestions. In the kitchen, the kettle was boiling. An honest calm descended on the house, and in the darkness of the room, Ludovina sat, saying nothing, as if crushed by what lay ahead: the discomfort, the poor food, her father's bad temper, the maid ruling the roost, everything that awaited her and everything she had lost, and she cursed her own ill fortune at having fallen into the arms of a man she didn't love, who gave her no pleasure – and for reasons that she herself could not fathom. Had it been mere foolishness, or because she had nothing else to do? No, even she did not know why.

V

The following morning, Godofredo was woken abruptly by a

ray of sun coming in through the window. He raised himself up on one elbow and blinked, astonished to find himself on a sofa, fully dressed and with his boots on. Then the memory of his misfortune fell upon his heart like a stone, and a black crêpe veil seemed to enfold everything. The previous evening, after Neto had left, he had lain down on the sofa, mortally tired, and fallen at once into a deep, heavy sleep. He sat up properly. A grave silence filled both house and street; it was barely six o'clock. The bedroom was in the same disorderly state as the night before, with the suitcase abandoned in the middle of the room, and Ludovina's peignoir thrown down on the chaise longue. He stared at that peignoir for a long time, and at the large bed in which no one had slept, with its two pillows lying next to each other. Then, as he had before, he walked through the house: in the dining room, the same cloth was on the table and upon it stood a forgotten candle, which had melted down and burned out in the candlestick. When he came to the parlour, however, he was gripped by cowardice and did not even dare touch the door curtain. He returned to the bedroom, sat down again on the sofa, hands hanging limp, gaze vacant, not knowing what to do at that early-morning hour, when the city was still asleep. Ludovina would probably be sleeping too. And he recalled the mornings on which he used to wake early, slip quietly out of bed and open the window a crack while she slept on, her hair caught up in a net, the lace trim of her nightdress touching her neck, and her long, dark eyelashes casting a shadow on her cheek. In the bright light, the still-made bed sent a chill through him, a feeling of hopelessness. He was filled with an immense sadness that dissolved his very bones and made him feel like lying down on the sofa again and simply dying. And the idea of death that had so haunted him yesterday returned, sliding into his mind as gently as a caress.

But in a few hours' time everything would be decided; perhaps he really was a dead man in waiting. He was due to meet the other man at eleven o'clock. His heart beat faster at the thought and he found it impossible to imagine Machado in any other pose than the one in which he had surprised him the previous evening, with his arm about Ludovina's waist. Drawing lots as to who should commit suicide, which had seemed so natural the night before, now frightened him a little. How strange that he, Alves, of Rua de São Bento – which now lay gilded by the morning sun – should have had such an idea, a tragic idea worthy of a far more impetuous heart than his. And he was filled with anxiety. What would the other man say to such a proposal? What if he refused? Other more finicky difficulties occurred to him. How exactly would they draw lots? With blank pieces of paper? And he was suddenly gripped by the fear that, confronted by such a wild proposal, the other man might laugh. If he did, he would slap him. But, how *could* he refuse? He was a man of honour! In a matter of hours, he would know his rival's response, but he did not want to think about that. The idea of drawing lots kept him occupied, almost deadened the pain, and gave him a sense of pride in himself, so that the situation seemed less ridiculous – and he preferred not to think about anything that diminished the importance of his plan.

Then he heard footsteps in the kitchen; the maids were up and about. Outside, a murmur of noise was gradually growing in strength, street cries and carts, the stirrings of a city waking up to a new day. And then, gradually, he resumed his daily routine, buttoned up his newly laundered shirt and sharpened his razor. But the sight of that large suitcase in the room troubled him. It suddenly occurred to him that he needed to make his will. Motionless before the mirror, with half his face covered in shaving soap, he pondered that thought, and the fact of standing there thinking about his last will and testament filled him with a kind of horror. All the ideas that had seemed so easy and natural to him during last night's fever, now, in the clear light of day, as he performed his *toilette*, seemed unnaturally cold and false, repugnant to the positive side of his nature.

At eight o'clock, the door bell rang. He went to listen. He could hear two women's voices out on the landing. Then the maid came in, and he asked who it was. Senhor Neto's maidservant, she said. And he didn't dare ask anything more, not even to find out what she wanted.

Then it was time for breakfast, which he devoured. He even asked for the ham to be brought in, and when the maid reappeared, she told him that the mistress would be sending for her luggage that night. He said nothing, but felt a growing dislike for Margarida, who seemed still to take her mistress's part, receiving her messages and acting as her confidante. When he noticed that the sugar bowl was missing, he was excessively harsh with her, threatening to put her out in the street.

Afterwards, on hearing Margarida muttering angrily in the corridor, he yelled:

'Keep the noise down!'

His heart pounded furiously whenever he thought of meeting the other man. Terrified of going out into the street, in case people were already talking about his misfortune, he ordered the maid to summon him a cab. She took her time. The clock ticked on. Drawing on his gloves, he paced nervously, almost feverishly, back and forth between window and door, and it seemed to him that the ground on which he walked was so soft that it gave beneath his feet. Finally, the carriage arrived. He went downstairs, his throat tight with anxiety. His voice almost quavered when he gave the driver the address of his office. The carriage positively flew along, and as his anxiety descended down into his stomach, so his breakfast rose up towards his throat. At last, he reached the office. He was in such a terrible state of nerves that he had to fumble in his pocket for a coin with which to pay the driver.

The office was still sleeping in the great Sunday silence, and as Alves pushed open the green baize door, the clock was striking eleven o'clock in its familiar sad, cavernous tones. He ran to his office, and it felt as if he had not been there for centuries and that the furniture and the order of things were all subtly altered. The flowers in the vase had withered.

A sudden change of mood came over him. Seeing that furniture, the two companionable desks side by side, and, remembering their years of friendship and trust, he was filled with a furious rage against Machado. And the things themselves accompanied him in his anger. Yes, Machado was a villain who properly deserved death. And every chair, the very walls, all imbued with the same commercial honesty as the room itself, silently condemned Machado for his betrayal.

Then came the sound of light footsteps outside: Machado.

Godofredo instinctively took refuge behind his desk, riffling through papers with tremulous hands, not daring to look up.

The door opened, and there stood Machado, as pale as death, one hand clutching his hat and cane, the other thrust into his trouser pocket, where it made a bulge like a fist.

Godofredo did not see this at first, not daring even to glance at him; his gaze flicked here and there, as he groped for something to say, something deep and dignified. Finally, with an effort, he faced Machado and immediately noticed that hand in the pocket; he started back, fearing a weapon, an attack. Machado understood and slowly withdrew his hand from his pocket, then went to place his hat and cane on the desk. Trembling in his haste and desire to say something, Godofredo managed to stammer:

'After what happened yesterday, we cannot continue to be friends.'

Machado, whose face was contorted in an expression of pain, closed his eyes and gave a sigh of relief. He had expected some terrible, violent attack, and Godofredo's moderation, his sad regret for a friendship betrayed, both shocked and impressed him. He would have liked, at that moment, to throw himself into his partner's arms; instead, he responded with genuine emotion, a lump in his throat:

'Unfortunately, yes…'

Then Godofredo gestured to him to sit down. Head bowed, Machado perched on the edge of the sofa. Godofredo sat down heavily, like an inert mass, on the stool next to his desk. A brief but deep silence reigned, made more intense by the quiet Sunday street dozing in the heat outside. Godofredo ran one tremulous hand over his face, searching for the right words to say.

Machado waited, his eyes fixed on the rug.

'A duel between us is impossible,' Godofredo said at last.

Machado blurted out:

'I am entirely at your disposal.'

'Impossible!' repeated Godofredo. 'We would be a laughing stock, especially given the duels one hears about nowadays. Ridiculous. In our position, we simply cannot hold a duel. A duel between two business partners? We would be the laughing-stock of Lisbon.'

And he was filled momentarily with the idea of them as

partners; the years during which they had worked together rose up before Godofredo, and he had never felt Machado's villainy so intensely as he did then, seeing him sitting in that office, where they had worked together for three years. He said:

'There are no words for your villainy…'

He had stood up, his voice had grown stronger, and his sense of being a friend betrayed lent to his voice a crushing dignity and solemnity. He spoke softly but firmly, almost hurling his words at Machado. He had known him since he was a child; he had helped him early on in his career; he had made him his partner, his friend. He had opened the doors of his house to him and welcomed him almost like a brother.

'And what did you do behind my back? You dishonoured me!'

Machado also stood up, a pained look on his face, wanting to put an end to this torture.

'I know, I know,' he stammered, 'and I'm ready to make amends in whatever way you choose.'

Excited now, Godofredo blurted out his idea:

'The only way to make amends is for one of us to die. A duel would be absurd. We must draw lots as to which of us should kill himself.'

These dread words, once spoken, struck him as strange and incoherent; even the furniture seemed to reject them, but he had spoken them now and felt relieved, having freed his soul of the idea that had so troubled and tormented him the previous night.

Machado stared at him, wide-eyed.

'What do you mean "draw lots"?'

He appeared not to understand. The idea of drawing lots to decide who should commit suicide seemed to him grotesque, mad.

When Godofredo remained standing by the desk, saying nothing, merely fiddling with his moustache, Machado exclaimed:

'Are you serious?'

It was Godofredo's turn to stare at Machado in bewilderment. He had feared this might happen. Machado found his idea absurd and was refusing to have anything to do with it. His anger grew, as if he could see his chance for revenge slipping from his grasp.

'You ran away yesterday when I found you *in flagrante;* you fled like a coward, and now you want to flee again.'

Deathly pale, Machado shouted back:

'Flee from what?'

He was filled with a silent rage that set his eyes glinting. He had found the litany of accusations hurled at him irritating, and now Godofredo was proposing some absurd form of suicide pact. It was insulting, and he would not stand for it. He said again:

'Flee from what? I'm not running away from anything.'

'Fine, then,' said Godofredo, slamming his hand down on the desk, 'we'll draw lots right now to decide which of us is to disappear!'

Machado stared at him for a moment, as if he were ready to strangle him, then he snatched up his hat and cane, and in a cutting, determined voice, said:

'I'm perfectly prepared to give you satisfaction for the wrong I've done you and to pay with my blood, but it has to be done in a normal, sensible fashion, with four witnesses, with swords or pistols, as you wish, and at a distance of your choosing, a duel to the death, if you want. I am at your disposal. I will be at home all day today and tomorrow, and will wait for you there. But I refuse to have any truck with the kind of mad idea you are proposing. And that's all I have to say.'

He left, slamming the door, and for a while, his furious footsteps could be heard outside; then the great silence returned. Godofredo was left alone amid the sad ruins of his grand idea, feeling humiliated, confused, angry, his head throbbing, and not knowing what to do next.

VI

Finally, just as Machado had done, he snatched up his hat and left the office. He was in such a daze that he was already halfway down Rua do Ouro when he realised that he had forgotten to lock the office door. He turned back, and this appeared to put some order into his ideas. He was determined now to fight Machado in a duel to the death; the only thing in the world that would satisfy him would be to see him lying at his feet, with a bullet through his heart. The man had dishonoured him, stolen his wife's love, and had the nerve to call him mad! This particularly enraged him because he had a vague sense himself that his notion of drawing lots to see which of them should commit suicide *was* slightly mad! Even if it was, though, Machado should not have said so; he should simply have resigned himself to accepting the satisfaction being asked of him. But he hadn't, he had demanded to make amends in a normal, sensible fashion. Fine, so be it; they would fight with pistols, only one of which would be loaded, and they would fire them at almost point-blank range. Then it would still be a matter of chance, of luck, leaving everything in God's just hands.

These were the thoughts occupying him as he walked briskly to the Rossio, where his close friend, Carvalho, lived. Carvalho had been director of the customs and excise office in Cabo Verde and had married well. Godofredo would go to him first and tell him everything, putting his trust in their longstanding friendship; then he would go and see another good friend, Teles Medeiros, a wealthy society man with considerable experience in such matters of honour; indeed, one room of his house was filled with a whole panoply of foils.

A clock was striking midday, and the July sun was beating down; the closed shops, the people in their Sunday best, the carriages in the square taking shelter in the shade, all added to the sense of heat and inertia. The blue sky was dimmed by a subtle layer of dust, and even the sound of the bells hung heavy on the soft air. As Godofredo was going up the steps to Carvalho's house, he met his friend coming down, looking very cool and pleased with himself in his new pale cheviot wool suit, and pulling on a pair of pearl-grey gloves. Shocked by Godofredo's evident distress, he immediately turned round again and went back inside, ushering his friend into a small study, where there was a bookcase and a long wicker chaise longue in the form of a day bed. In the next room, someone was playing the piano, a fast-paced waltz that made the whole house vibrate.

Carvalho then drew the door curtain and closed the open window before asking Godofredo what was the matter.

Godofredo put his hat down on one corner of the table and poured out his heart.

At the words 'sofa' and 'arm about her waist', Carvalho, who was slowly removing his gloves, stood dumbstruck in the middle of the room, then ran to draw the door curtain still more closely as if he feared that a faint indecent whiff of that tale of betrayal might leak out into the rest of the apartment. Carvalho listened eagerly to Godofredo's account, but it was so garbled that. at first, Carvalho didn't realise who the man in question was, understanding only that Machado had been present; when he learned that Machado had, in fact, been the man sitting on the sofa, he clapped his hands and gave a cry of horror:

'How despicable!'

'He was like a brother to me!' moaned Godofredo, shaking his fists. 'And this is how he repays me. No, the man has to die. I want a duel to the death!'

A flicker of disquiet crossed Carvalho's face. Now he understood. Godofredo had not come purely to unburden himself, he had come looking for a witness, a second; and Carvalho was immediately seized by a bureaucrat's fear of the law, a fear of compromising himself. His egotism rebelled against the violent, troubling things that he could sense lay ahead. He tried to make light of the matter, to find explanations. If that was all Godofredo had seen, if he had come across them simply sitting together in the room, perhaps it was a joke, a moment's foolishness.

Godofredo felt feverishly in his pockets. In the other room, the piano was quieter now, more tentative, as if the player were trying to remember a forgotten melody. Suddenly, a snatch of music from *Rigoletto* burst forth, a sobbing, mournful tune. And having at last found the letter, Godofredo set it before Carvalho, who quietly read it out:

'Ah, love of my life, what an afternoon that was…'

And as if those words, when read out by someone else, sounded even viler than when he himself had read them, Godofredo could contain himself no longer and, raising his voice, he cried:

'No, this must be paid for in blood! It's a duel to the death or nothing.'

Feeling most uneasy, Carvalho urged him to be quiet. And when the piano stopped, he listened for a while, fearing that his friend's cry had been heard.

'It's Mariana,' he said, indicating the next room. 'It's best she doesn't know about this for the moment.'

Then he slowly re-read the letter, stroking the paper, turning it over and holding it in his fingers with excited curiosity.

Godofredo was fumbling in his pockets again, regretting not having brought the other letters with him too, because there were others still worse. And gripped now by the desire to prove to Carvalho that his wife was no better than a whore, he quoted whole lines from memory, lines that proved Ludovina's folly and shamelessness.

'Besides, he didn't deny a word of it!'

'You mean you've spoken to him?'

After a pause, Godofredo completed his confession, telling Carvalho about his meeting with Machado and about his proposal that they should draw lots to decide which of them should commit suicide. As if shattered by these revelations and astonished that such terrible, violent things could actually happen and be spoken about there in his quiet Rossio home, Carvalho slumped down onto the chaise longue, where he sat, wide-eyed.

When Godofredo commented that Machado had found his idea absurd, Carvalho burst out:

'He's quite right! It's arrant madness!'

And he scrabbled in the air of that cramped study for a more appropriate word to describe Godofredo's idea, but could not improve on 'madness'. He concluded by saying that it was the kind of thing one might read about in an adventure story.

Godofredo said: 'I'm demanding that the duel be fought

with pistols, only one of which will be loaded, the pistols to be chosen and fired at random, so it'll come to the same thing…'

Carvalho started out of his seat.

'Only one loaded pistol? Chosen at random? But that's murder! No, I'm afraid you can't count on me for that. There's no reason for it, and even if there were, I certainly wouldn't want to be involved!'

Finding himself thus abandoned, Godofredo rebelled. Was his best friend going to let him down in the midst of this terrible crisis? Who, then, could he turn to? Who would defend his honour?

Carvalho took offence. He spoke again of murder, crime and prison, concluding:

'What if you had invited me to set fire to the Bank of Portugal, would you have expected me to agree to that as well?'

Godofredo tried to explain that this wasn't the same thing at all; their voices rose and mingled, and suddenly the piano fell silent, silencing them as well. Then the conversation next door became louder; voices were raised, there was an altercation, in which the words 'white petticoat', 'you slattern' and 'but Madame never said anything about that' were angrily exchanged. Carvalho listened for a moment, then shrugged. It must be some new dereliction of duty on the part of the maid, a shameless hussy, who had been with them a month, but could do nothing right. When he heard a door slam, he could not resist going to see what was happening.

Godofredo felt a sudden wave of weariness wash over him. Ever since the previous day, his nerves had been wound as tightly as the strings on a highly-tuned violin. Everything had seemed easy then and his vengeance assured. He had now received two unpleasant setbacks, one after the other. Machado had rejected the idea of suicide by lottery, and Carvalho wanted nothing to do with a duel to the death. Something inside him was slackening, as if his soul were growing weary of keeping up that pose of grim revenge for hours on end. He again began to feel the onset of a headache, the headache that had been threatening since last night. He sat down on the sofa, his head in his hands, and gave a deep sigh.

Carvalho came back in, red-faced and excited. There had been a scene, and he had dismissed the maid. He then began ranting on about how impossible it was to find a decent maid nowadays, how they were all a bunch of filthy, shameless, thieving slatterns. How he longed for the black maids who had worked for him in Africa, for there was nothing like a black maid...

'Anyway, what do you think of this whole business?' cried an increasingly discouraged Godofredo.

Carvalho shrugged.

'It's best to leave things as they are, with your wife living in her father's house, you in yours, and see how things work out.'

Then, filled with something resembling remorse, he tried to show how generous he was really and added:

'But in order to salvage your honour, you can count on me for an ordinary duel, with swords or even pistols. That would be fine, but I'm not getting involved in any tragedies.'

Godofredo picked up his hat and said:

'Let's go and see what Medeiros has to say.'

Carvalho was rather put out. He had been planning to spend the day at Pedrouços with his wife, at his father-in-law's house. It was his brother-in-law's birthday. But, given the circumstances, his friend's needs came first.

'All right, but first let me warn Mariana that I can't go to

Pedrouços.'

He soon returned, rather irritably drawing on his gloves. Halfway down the stairs, he stopped and turned to Godofredo, who was following him:

'You do know that my wife is expecting, don't you? Any shock could prove fatal, and if she finds out that I'm going to be a second at a duel, well... It's no joke, you know. But let's go and see Medeiros; after all, that's what friends are for.'

Once out in the street, they hailed a cab, because Medeiros lived some way away, beyond Estrela. The cab was almost new, well-sprung, comfortable and quiet. This put Carvalho in a better humour, and he leaned back and finished buttoning his gloves. For some time, they said nothing. Then, as the cab was crossing Rua do Loreto, Carvalho was suddenly filled with curiosity and asked Godofredo for more details. What had Ludovina said? What had Neto said? Briefly and wearily, Godofredo told him. Carvalho disapproved of the allowance of thirty *mil réis*. It was tantamount to rewarding infamy. But seeing Godofredo biting his lip as if fighting back tears, he murmured:

'Ah, life can be cruel!'

And they exchanged not another word until they reached Medeiros' house. When they rang the bell, the servant informed them that Senhor Medeiros was still in bed. Carvalho marched up the stairs and burst noisily into Medeiros' bedroom, calling him a sluggard and a debauchee. Behind him, in the dark, Godofredo was stumbling over various bits of furniture, and in the curtained gloom, Medeiros' tetchy voice asked who they thought they were, invading his room like that. And when the curtains were drawn back, he screamed and buried himself beneath the sheets, unable to bear the sudden brightness. Finally, though, he revealed his puffy face, still heavy with sleep; then he stretched, propped himself on one elbow and took a cigarette from the bedside table.

Carvalho sat at the foot of the bed and, for a moment, they discussed Medeiros' slothful habits, with Medeiros explaining that he had only got to bed at five that morning.

Then Carvalho said:

'We're here about a very serious matter.'

Medeiros interrupted him by calling for his servant, wanting to know if a letter had been delivered that morning. The boy had it in his pocket. Medeiros, his hair all dishevelled, sat down on the bed, tore open the envelope, read the letter at a glance, gave a sigh of relief and placed it under his pillow.

'I nearly got caught red-handed yesterday. Another second and, well, if her husband had chanced to come into the kitchen, which is right next to the front door, then he would have found out just how "faithful" his Marta really is. Oh, I had such a fright!'

Carvalho and Godofredo exchanged glances, and Carvalho said:

'Well, it's something of the kind that brings us here today…' adding: 'Alves has had an unfortunate experience…'

And faced by Medeiros' wide-eyed gaze, Godofredo's throat grew tight again with a sense of his own ridiculousness, as a member of the grotesque tribe of betrayed husbands, who could not enter his own house without some lover skedaddling out of the back door. It was the same throughout the city, in which every infamous corner was full of lovers either fleeing or being waylaid. He had waylaid his wife's lover, and what if that other husband had gone into the kitchen and caught Marta's escaping lover? What a terrible day yesterday had been! It seemed to him that the whole of Lisbon was swept up in that dance, with lovers slinking off or husbands catching them, a *chassez-croisez* performed around women's skirts. He was overwhelmed by weariness, and by a horror of having to tell his story yet again. However, Medeiros' eyes and face were waiting, and so in the end he said with an exhausted air:

'It happened yesterday. I caught Ludovina with Machado.'

'Good God!' cried Medeiros, sitting bolt upright in bed.

And stubbing out his cigarette and quickly taking up another, he insisted on knowing all the details. In talkative mood now, Carvalho took over, enjoying his role and speaking with all the confidence of a husband married to a wealthy dullard whom no one had been tempted to seduce. He recounted the whole sorry tale, while Godofredo sat hunched on a chair, nodding and still clutching his tall hat.

'Show him the letter,' Carvalho said when he had finished.

Godofredo took the letter from his pocket, and Medeiros read it out loud, and for the second time that day, Godofredo heard his wife's words in the voice of another man: 'Ah, love of my life, what an afternoon that was…'

And still in his nightshirt, Medeiros repeated those words and fumbled with the paper, turning it this way and that, just as Carvalho had, inflamed by the memory of Ludovina's dark eyes and regal body.

Then he was filled with a sudden terrible rage against Machado. What a rogue! Not that she was entirely innocent, of course. When a woman takes a fancy to someone, you can't expect all men to be like Joseph of Egypt! But one should certainly draw the line at the wife of a close friend, let alone a business partner…

'This calls for blood,' he said, excitedly jumping off the bed and into the middle of the room in his nightshirt and slippers.

His courage restored, Godofredo cried:

'I wanted a duel to the death, but Carvalho disagrees.'

Carvalho appealed to his friend Medeiros. Could one have a duel in which only one of the pistols was loaded and then chosen at random?

Medeiros stared at them, horrified. Of course not. Besides, there was no reason for such a thing.

This was the second time Godofredo had been told that there was 'no reason' and he burst out angrily, waving his arms:

'What do you mean "no reason"? What then do you consider to be sufficient reason for two men to kill each other?'

'If one of them spat in the other's face, for example,' said Medeiros authoritatively, as he hurriedly combed his hair.

Godofredo tried to argue, but Medeiros spun round, comb in hand, and said firmly:

'Even if there were a reason, you certainly wouldn't get me to agree to be involved in such an affair.'

'You see?' exclaimed Carvalho triumphantly. 'What did I tell you? No one would be willing to take on a responsibility like that. I certainly wouldn't, not with my wife expecting. A fine mess that would be!'

For a moment, Alves seemed utterly crestfallen. And yet what he was actually feeling was a twinge of relief, as if some of the previous night's indecision had vanished and been replaced by a kind of resolution. It was decided now that there would be no drawing of lots, no random choices, that no one would die; and in the midst of the emotional turmoil into which he had been plunged up until then, this provided a fixed point, a basis, a decision on which he could rest. It had not been his decision, but the decision reached by his best friends, basing themselves on cool reason. And yet, even though they had rejected the idea that either he or Machado should die, something still had to be done.

'What would you advise me to do, then? I can't just sit here doing nothing.'

Standing in the middle of the room in his large slippers, with his scrawny shins on view, Medeiros said very solemnly:

'Would you be prepared to place your honour in my hands?'

Of course Godofredo would, that was why he was there.

'Right,' exclaimed Medeiros. 'Don't give the matter another thought. Leave it to us. We will arrange everything.'

And he disappeared into a small adjacent room, where they could hear him brushing his teeth, gargling and making large splashing noises in the basin.

Still not entirely satisfied, Godofredo went over to the room, asking for more information.

'You don't need to know anything more,' roared Medeiros, vigorously washing himself with sponge and water. 'We don't know what's going to happen yet either. First, we have to see Machado and find out what he has to say, and talk to his seconds and so on. You go home now and don't leave the house until we arrive. And we'll need a cab for all these toings and froings. I'll have Domingos brush my black frock coat and my black trousers. This calls for sombre wear.'

When he heard this, Carvalho looked down at his own pale cheviot wool suit, but he wasn't one for such sartorial proprieties: a man could decently go anywhere as long as he had on a clean shirt.

Godofredo was still pacing thoughtfully up and down. In the end, he told Carvalho what was troubling him.

'You need to present him with clear conditions. I would prefer pistols at twenty paces…'

'Leave it all to Medeiros,' said Carvalho.

And Medeiros, who reappeared at that point, towel in hand and his hair all wet, added:

'You may understand about business matters, Alves, but when it comes to matters of honour, I'm your man. All you have to do now is wait for us to tell you what's going to happen – time, place and weapons. You don't even have to worry about a doctor. I'll ask Gomes to come along to give any necessary treatment. He'd be sure to keep a cool head if one of you should be badly wounded.'

Godofredo felt a shiver run down his spine, and his heart contracted. Beside him, Carvalho was saying:

'You go off home now. You've probably got papers and what-not to put in order…'

He did not mention the words 'last will and testament', but that was clearly what he meant. And this irritated Godofredo. True, he was the one who wanted a proper duel that would end in death, but there they were, his two best and closest friends, one already speculating about serious wounds and the other hustling him out of the door to go home and write his will. They seemed to him crass and unnecessarily cruel. He left without a word and, bruised in body and soul, flung himself into a cab, where he had this one deep thought:

'Is it for this that people get married? Is this why people want a family?'

VII

At six o'clock that evening, a beslippered Godofredo was sitting in his study, having just finished putting seals on a whole bundle of papers, when the door bell rang, and his two friends were announced. Despite his scorn for etiquette, Carvalho had been home to change his clothes and donned a black frock coat; both men looked extremely serious.

Medeiros, dressed impeccably now and with his moustache waxed, sat down on the sofa in the room into which they had been shown by the maid and began slowly drawing off his black gloves, his eyes fixed on Godofredo.

'You are doubtless bursting with curiosity, but for the moment, unfortunately, nothing has been decided.'

Godofredo, white-faced, had his eyes glued on Medeiros and seemed to breathe more easily at this news. Then he grew angry. What did they mean 'nothing had been decided'? Was the villain refusing to give him satisfaction?

Carvalho said:

'No, not at all. Credit where credit is due, Machado is quite prepared to fight a duel.'

'So?'

'It's the seconds who aren't keen,' explained Medeiros. 'Let me explain.'

It was a long story, which Medeiros recounted, savouring every detail. They had spoken to Machado, who promised that two friends of his would be at Medeiros' house at four o'clock. The friends duly turned up: Nunes Vidal, whom he knew very well, and who was experienced in matters of honour, and Albertinho Cunha, who said very little and was there as Vidal's assistant. They exchanged greetings in a serious, but friendly fashion, then came straight to the point: Nunes Vidal declared at once that, in principle, Senhor Machado was ready to accept any and all of the conditions proposed by Senhor Alves. However, he, Nunes Vidal, and his friend Cunha, understood that, in any such conflict, the duty of the seconds was, above all, to seek peace and reconciliation. And while, on the one hand, their friend, Senhor Machado, out of an excess of pride and a sense of honour, was prepared to let himself be killed, they, his seconds, who had taken it upon themselves to safeguard his interests, were there not only to avoid, as far as possible, any harm coming to their friend in a duel, but also to avoid any potentially damaging scandal attaching to his name.

'And all this was very well and clearly put,' added Medeiros. 'Yes, I really like Vidal.'

'A very talented young man,' murmured Carvalho.

'Anyway, Vidal ended by saying that, all things considered, they did not feel there was sufficient reason for a duel with pistols.'

'Again, insufficient reason!' Godofredo exploded. 'Damn it, what does that ass think Machado could have done to me that was any worse?'

Medeiros silenced him with a gesture.

'Now don't get upset. That's precisely what I told him. Vidal may be a bright lad, but I said my piece too. Ask Carvalho.'

'You were better than any lawyer,' said Carvalho.

'And then what did Vidal say?' cried Godofredo.

Vidal said that there was no reason for blood to be spilled because what had passed between Machado and the lady in question was merely a flirtation.

Godofredo sprang angrily to his feet, and Medeiros followed suit:

'Calm down. I laid it all out before them. I told them that you had found the two of them *in flagrante*, I told them about the letter – "what an afternoon that was" and the rest. I presented them with all the necessary facts to prove to them that adultery had taken place. Isn't that right, Carvalho?'

'Absolutely.'

'I told them clearly: my principal, my friend Alves, I said, is, in the fullest sense of the word, a husband who… well, who demands satisfaction. Isn't that right, Carvalho?'

Carvalho nodded.

'But Nunes proved me wrong. He had read the letters too, and Machado had told him his side of the story. After much discussion and thought, he had reached the conclusion that the "affair" had never got beyond being a flirtation.'

A silence fell. Godofredo was pacing briskly up and down, his hands in his pockets. Carvalho was absent-mindedly examining a painting depicting Leda and the swan. Suddenly, Godofredo stopped pacing and said quietly, enunciating every word:

'I saw them embracing on that very sofa. What does Nunes have to say to that?'

'That is the one point,' exclaimed Medeiros, 'the one point that cannot be denied, because you saw it with your own eyes. But Machado explained it all to Nunes, and he, in turn, explained it to us. It was just a bit of fun apparently; he was simply tickling her.'

'And what about the letter and those words "what an afternoon that was"?' asked Godofredo.

'According to Nunes that refers to a trip you made to Belém together. Did you go to Belém?'

Godofredo thought for a moment. Yes, it was true, the three of them had made a trip to Belém.

'There you are, you see. She was merely remembering the pleasure of going there together – an outing, a lark.'

'So that's it, is it?' cried Godofredo. 'Nothing happened, and I have to swallow the insult?'

Medeiros rose indignantly to his feet. What did he take him for? Had Alves not placed his honour in his and Carvalho's hands? He had. Then how could he imagine that they, his friends, would leave him to wallow in the mud like a wretch?

'Yes, but...' began Alves.

'But what? Of course, there has to be a duel. And that was

what was decided. A mere flirtation isn't enough to justify a duel with pistols, but since Senhor Machado has no right to flirt with your wife, there is every motive for a duel with swords, an altogether simpler affair. We're going to meet them again at my house at eight o'clock and arrange everything.'

'And we haven't much time to spare,' said Carvalho, taking out his watch. 'It's half past six already, and we still haven't had dinner. I'm starving...'

Godofredo invited them to dine with him. Besides, on the assumption that they would arrive at around dinner time, he had already ordered the cook to prepare more meat.

'There'll only be a mouthful of roast,' he said, 'but that's more than enough when one is on campaign. And we are, after all, on a war footing...'

This was the first time he had smiled since the previous day, but he was cheered by having his friends dine with him, thus avoiding the solitude he so dreaded.

And dinner turned out to be a jolly affair. They had agreed not to talk about the duel or the reason for the duel, but from the first course onwards, whenever Margarida was out of the room, they all made vague allusions to the topic. Finally, Godofredo told Margarida to return only when he rang the bell, and then there was no stopping the conversation. Godofredo described how he had met Ludovina, their courtship and their wedding day. Then he spoke about Machado, but without any trace of anger, even going so far as to say that he was 'a young man of spirit'. He used to collect Machado from school when he was just a boy, and sometimes take him to the theatre. The memories brought a lump to his throat, and he said he would rather speak no more about it. He rang the bell, and Margarida brought in the roast. There was a brief silence, then Medeiros praised the Colares wine. Carvalho, who used to drink Colares wine when he lived in Cabo Verde, recalled another duel for which he had been called on to act as a second, and as soon as Margarida had left the room again, he told his friends the story. It had been a similar case to that of Alves, except that the woman had been black. Medeiros found this incredible. But Carvalho, eyes shining, spoke in warm praise of black women:

'Once you get used to them, you won't want any other kind. They're all woman!'

'Can we, please, not talk about women,' said Godofredo.

And in that request, accompanied by a faint smile, there was a kind of resignation to his misfortune, the beginnings of a desire to enjoy life, the company of his friends, and his business concerns, without the upsets that anything involving the female sex invariably brings with it. They spoke instead about Nunes. Medeiros was pleased that such a serious, experienced, honourable young man like Nunes should be in charge. He had been afraid at first that Machado might take it into his head to choose as his second that idiot Sigismundo, in whose company he was always to be seen. And this brought the conversation back to Machado. Enlivened by the wine, Medeiros confessed that he had already had his revenge on Machado, for he had been the lover of a French woman who, at the time, had also been Machado's mistress. He went on to talk about himself and his conquests, and returned to the previous evening's escapade, when he was nearly caught in the kitchen. Carvalho had a similar tale to tell, one that had happened in Tomar. He'd jumped out of a window and landed on a pile of manure. Pinheiro, a friend of his – not the thin one, the one with the pockmarked face – had met with an even worse fate. He had been forced to hide in a pig sty for six whole hours. He nearly died. He still turned white as a sheet whenever he saw a pig. Carvalho and Medeiros between them went on to tell tale after adulterous tale. As a decent, married man, Godofredo had no such anecdotes; his life had been entirely domestic and devoid of extra-marital affairs, and so he listened, sipping his coffee, enjoying that cheerful end to the supper, and occasionally smiling.

Touched by the warm breath of youth, he even remarked philosophically:

'Far better to amuse ourselves after our own fashion than to let other people amuse themselves at our expense.'

It was nearly eight o'clock. Carvalho began to pull on his black gloves. Godofredo suggested that he accompany them; he could hide in Medeiros' bedroom while the discussion went on in the living room; that way they wouldn't have to go to the trouble of returning to his house to report on their conclusions. Initially, Carvalho felt that this went counter to etiquette, but in the end he agreed, since it did not seem a very grave offence.

They called a cab and, with all three of them squashed inside, they set off to Estrela.

At Medeiros' house, the servant had already lit the chandelier, and the three men had barely gone up the stairs when the bell rang. Machado's seconds had arrived punctually at eight o'clock. While Godofredo went and hid in the bedroom, the others went into the living room, whence came a murmur of voices. In the darkness, Godofredo did not dare to summon Medeiros' servant, and so he groped about on the table and the dressing table for a box of matches. He found none, but his fingers did find a door curtain, which he drew back, and there before him was a crack of light from the door, beyond which he could hear men speaking. On the other side lay the living room, where the discussion was taking place. He stepped forward, but collided with a jug, which toppled over with a sound of spilling water. He stood motionless for a moment, then squelched closer to the door and put his ear to the keyhole. Silence had fallen, although he couldn't understand why. He tried to peer through the keyhole, but all he could see was a piece of mirror in which was reflected the light from a candlestick. Suddenly, the light disappeared, and he could see only blackness, doubtless the back of one of the men present. Then a voice spoke more loudly. It was Medeiros saying something about how it all seemed to him quite conclusive. Then he heard two other voices, which mingled and grew louder, although he could not make out what they were saying. Then another more formal voice said very clearly:

'Dignity above all else.'

Quite right, but his being there, eavesdropping, was hardly dignified. He felt his way back into the room and, having bumped into the sofa, sat down. There was no noise now, and in the room the air hung heavy. The darkness brought with it ideas of illness. The following day, he might be in just such a darkened room, prostrate on a bed; alone, with no one to care for him but Margarida. The thought filled him with horror. He recalled stories he had been told about wounds. A sword thrust felt cold at first, apparently; the pain came later and lasted a long time, during endless nights spent lying motionless on hot mattresses. Then he thought about everything that Nunes had said to Carvalho, that it was the first time Machado had embraced her, that it was just a bit of fun. What if that were true? She had said precisely that: it was the first time. Perhaps it was merely a flirtation, a dalliance. Should he forgive them? No. But it was hardly a motive for a duel. He need only banish Machado from his house. Other thoughts rushed in. Of late, Ludovina had been particularly affectionate towards him. Before, he had always been the one to make the first move... Lately, however, it had been she who, sometimes for no apparent reason, would fling her arms about his neck. Could he say definitely that she did not love him? No. She wasn't pretending; he wasn't that foolish; he could recognise genuine feeling. Why, then, had she allowed the other man to pay her court? Who knows? Coquetry, vanity perhaps... That did deserve punishment. No, he would never see her again, and he would fight Machado. Then it occurred to him that he had never used a sword, and Machado had given lessons in fencing. He was sure to be the one who was wounded. And the same terror filled his mind. He would not, he felt, be so afraid of a sudden death, a bullet through the heart, for example, but a serious wound confining him to bed for long, slow weeks at a time, with fever, inflammation, the danger of gangrene, that was horrible. His flesh crept and shrank at the very idea, but honour demanded it.

Suddenly, he heard voices and laughter out in the corridor, the cheerful sound of friends saying their goodbyes. His heart was beating fast. He had made his way over to the bedroom door. A light appeared. It was Medeiros bearing the candle with which he had shown the others to the door.

'It's all resolved,' he said, coming into the room.

Behind him, Carvalho was saying the same:

'Yes, it's all resolved.'

Godofredo, pale and trembling with nerves, was staring at them.

'There's to be no duel,' said Medeiros, putting the candlestick down on the table.

'Didn't I tell you?' exclaimed Carvalho, beaming. 'Common sense has prevailed.'

And it once again fell to Medeiros to recount what had happened during the discussions. Nunes Vidal had behaved like a true gentleman. He had begun by saying that if he were truly convinced that Machado had betrayed his business partner by committing the sin of adultery with his partner's wife, then he would never have got involved. As it was, however, if they insisted on a duel, then their terms as to time, place and choice of foils would be accepted unquestioningly. When they reached the appointed place, Machado would, like a gentleman, take up the sword and allow himself to be wounded. But then Nunes had appealed to them as men of honour and good sense.

'That's what he said, isn't it, Carvalho?'

'And men of the world too,' added Carvalho.

'Exactly, men of the world. He appealed to us, asking if it was right to allow a duel to take place when there was no good reason for it, especially given that, in a letter Nunes gave me to read, Machado had sworn on his sacred honour as a gentleman that Senhora Dona Ludovina was totally innocent. Yes, they had exchanged a few silly letters, but that was all, well, apart from that embrace of course. Besides, asked Nunes, what would be the effect of a duel? It would compromise Senhora Dona Ludovina, persuade people that an adulterous act really had taken place, make Senhor Alves look ridiculous and possibly harm the company.'

'And don't forget Nunes' dilemma,' said Carvalho.

'Of course, the dilemma,' cried Medeiros. 'Nunes put the dilemma thus: you are demanding a duel with swords; if adultery did take place, then a duel with swords is too little, and if there was no adultery, it's too much. And so we decided that there should be no duel at all.'

Godofredo said nothing, but was filled by a feeling of peace and serenity. The grand statements made by that honourable fellow Nunes almost convinced him that there really had been nothing more than a flirtation. He had even said that if he was convinced adultery had taken place, he would have no more to do with the matter, because he was a true gentleman. If it had been a mere flirtation, then there was no reason to fight, and this was an enormous relief to him; a thousand hideous ideas vanished to be replaced by thoughts of repose, peace and perhaps even happiness. He still wouldn't forgive his wife for the flirtation, and he would never again speak to Machado, but knowing that they had not actually betrayed him would make life less bitter.

It was a salve to his pride. He had shown himself to be an upright and honourable husband, dismissing his wife merely for exchanging glances with another man. Honour was thus saved, and his heart would suffer less.

It filled him with joy to be able to emerge at last from all those violent thoughts of death and go back to his usual routine, to his business, his friendships, his books. These same comforting thoughts, however, suddenly filled him with perturbation.

'What about Machado? I can't possibly speak to Machado again!'

Medeiros had discussed this point with Nunes. And Nunes had come up with a very sensible idea. This is what he said. Since there was now no reason to have a duel, there was no reason to end their business relationship either.

Godofredo protested:

'You mean that he'll just come into the office tomorrow as normal?'

'Who said anything about tomorrow? This, according to Nunes, is what Machado will do. Tomorrow he will write you an official letter, so that the bookkeeper and the cashier will see it, and in it he will explain that he is going abroad with his mother for a while and asks you to look after things in his absence. After a month or two, he will return, you will greet each other, sit down at your respective desks, discuss any business matters pending, and that will be an end of the matter. You will not, however, be on intimate terms any more, you will no longer treat each other as friends.'

And when Godofredo sat staring at the floor, thinking, his two friends immediately fell upon him:

'That will stop the mouths of the gossips,' said Carvalho.

'It will save you from ridicule,' said Medeiros.

'The firm will remain intact and united!'

'Your wife's reputation will be saved!'

'You won't have to lose an intelligent, hard-working partner.'

'Or, possibly, a friend.'

Godofredo was filled by a terrible weariness. His nerves slackened. He wanted never to think or speak again about this whole unpleasant business and to sleep peacefully once more. He gave in, allowed himself to be persuaded, and asked in heartfelt tones:

'And you truly believe that this is the best way to resolve the matter?'

'We do,' they said.

Moved almost to tears, Godofredo shook the hand, first, of one friend and then of the other.

'Thank you, Carvalho. Thank you, Medeiros.'

Then, in order to silence any malicious tongues, they all went off to the Passeio Público to watch the fireworks, stopping first at Café Martinho for an ice cream.

VIII

Thus began Godofredo's abominable new existence.

The weeks passed and Machado returned to occupy his desk in the office. Godofredo had greatly feared this encounter and thought it would prove impossible for them to spend their days beside each other, handling the same papers, connected by a thousand common interests, when they would both be thinking about that fateful ninth of July, and that scene on the sofa. In the end, though, everything passed off smoothly and without awkwardness.

On the eve of his return, Machado had written him a polite, almost humble letter, in which one could detect a certain note of sadness. In the letter, he said that he was now ready to resume work and would come to the office the following day, adding that he hoped their new working relationship would not be overshadowed by the past, but would be conducted with due respect and courtesy; he added, however, that he understood perfectly well the difficulties of this new situation and so would only remain in his position for a short time, just long enough to protect the dignity of all concerned and to silence any gossip, adding that he would leave the company as soon as he could safely do so without causing any scandal. On that day, Godofredo went to the office earlier than usual, and he did something very clever: he told the bookkeeper – in the cashier's presence – that there had been a slight difference of opinion between himself and Senhor Machado and, as result, their relationship had cooled slightly. These vague words were intended to avert any surprise or comment on the part of the bookkeeper when he saw them face to face, treating each other with curt politeness and addressing each other formally as Senhor Alves and Senhor Machado. The bookkeeper murmured something about 'being very sorry to hear it', and shortly afterwards, Machado appeared. It was a most disagreeable moment. For the rest of the day, neither man could concentrate on his work, and Machado's slightest movement – whether pulling out his handkerchief or walking across the room – awoke all kinds of unpleasant memories in Godofredo. Once or twice, he was filled by a violent desire to attack Machado verbally, accusing him of being the cause of all his current woes. He held back, however, although not without uttering the occasional heartfelt sigh.

Machado appeared both respectful and sad, and the two men barely exchanged a word. A kind of anxiety hovered in the air. And the foolish cashier only made matters worse by tiptoeing around as if he were in the house of a dying man.

Other similarly painful days followed, but, gradually, Machado's presence ceased to trouble Godofredo, and he was able to look at him without thinking of the sofa. They quickly got into a routine: the last to arrive would offer the other a polite 'Good morning', and, thereafter, they would speak only about business matters. When there was no work to be done, Machado would leave, while Godofredo stayed behind in the office reading the newspapers. And things continued in this frictionless fashion, because, deep down, Machado felt only esteem for kindly Alves, and Alves, despite himself, was still very fond of Machado, the lad he had known since he was a child. In vain did he say to himself that, outside of his role as business partner, Machado was an utter rogue; Machado's tone of voice and fine manners drew Alves to him.

So it was that, by early October, the tumultuous agitation that had taken over Godofredo's life and brought him weeks of sleepless nights had gradually dissipated. Ludovina was in

Ericeira with her father, and the memory of the moment when he had found her sitting on the yellow sofa – a memory that had, at first, been like an open wound in Godofredo's heart, irritated by the slightest movement, the slightest touch – was still a wound, but it had now healed over and was the source only of the kind of dull ache to which the body gradually becomes accustomed. The unpleasantness of meeting Machado again also faded, and in the office in Rua dos Douradores, they established a relationship that was cool, courteous and entirely bearable. However, that restoration of calm only made Godofredo more aware of every detail of the widower's existence that would now be his for ever, and he found in it only discomfort and sadness. At first, he considered leaving his house in Rua de São Bento and going to live in a hotel, but feared what other people might say. No one knew he was separated from his wife. They assumed she had gone with her father to the seaside and that Godofredo went to visit her there. And it was essential that he maintain that fiction. Besides, what would he do with their two servants? He was determined to maintain total secrecy regarding his misfortune, by keeping under lock and key, so to speak, the two people who knew about it and who were bound to him by the lure of an excellent position. And so he stayed in São Bento, but his life there was a hell. One by one, his beloved comforts disappeared, because, without a mistress to keep an eye on them, the two servants had become sloppy and complacent, aware that their master would not dismiss them because he depended on their silence. The day's torments began for Godofredo at nine o'clock. Getting them to bring him water so that he could shave was nigh on impossible; there was never any hot water to be had, because the cook got up late now and didn't even light the stove until ten. Then there was a further battle to get any breakfast, which, when it did come – hastily and badly prepared, and always the same – almost made him feel sick. Since August, they had been serving the same boiled eggs – either raw or overcooked – and the same blackened steaks, as tough as burnt leather. He would sit down and gaze in horror at his filthy, unwashed napkin. Ah, gone were the days when Ludovina herself would prepare him his boiled eggs, timing them with an hourglass! Then, there were always flowers on the table and beside his plate his regular newspapers – the *Diário de Notícias* and the *Jornal do Comércio* – which he would open and read, aware all the time of the rustle of her skirts, the warmth of her presence, the faint aroma of toilet water.

When he returned home at four o'clock, the remains of that wretched breakfast were still on the table, the gravy from the steaks congealed on the plate, the grouts from his tea still in the cup, while flies hovered over the whole sad, grubby mess, and on the floor lay several weeks' worth of crumbs. Every day, the servants seemed to manage to break something. And the end-of-the-month account was exorbitant, absurdly high. Twice he had encountered men on the stairs or visitors for the maids. His dirty washing lay in piles in corners, and when he did finally explode, rushing into the kitchen like a bomb about to go off, they didn't even reply, feigning a compunction which he found even more repulsive than an honestly insolent response. They bowed their heads, respectfully offered some ridiculous excuse, and then stayed in the kitchen giggling and drinking glasses of wine.

Worst of all, though, were the lonely evenings. He had always been very much a stay-at-home, choosing to raise the domestic drawbridge at nine o'clock, put on his slippers and savour his personal paradise. Normally, Ludovina would be there in the room with him, playing the piano, and he himself would light the lamps, as devoutly as someone preparing an altar, because he loved music; and then he would sit in an armchair, listening to her play, gazing at her long, thick, dark hair that hung in a state of charming, uncombed dishevelment. Certain pieces of music made him feel as if his heart were being caressed by something so soft and velvety they almost made him swoon, in particular a waltz called *Souvenir d'Andalousie*. It had been such a long time since he had last heard that waltz.

While the summer lasted, he went for his regular evening walk, but even the spectacle of the streets was a reminder of his lost happiness. The sight of a lady in a pale dress standing on a balcony, enjoying the cool, spoke to him of his now empty home, in which there was no rustle of skirts, as did a window from which emerged the sounds of a piano and the discreet glow of someone's peaceful soirée. It was then, feeling weary and with his boots dusty, that he felt his solitude most poignantly.

The worst evenings, though, were those he spent in the Passeio Público, to which he was drawn by his horror of solitude; but being alone among people, beneath the trees along the gas-lit avenues, seeing all those men arm-in-arm with their wives, was more painful to him by far than his cold, deserted room at home and the abandoned piano.

Things only got worse with the onset of winter, with November proving to be a very rainy month. Godofredo would return from the office and, after a very plain dinner, which he ate as quickly as possible, he would wander from room to room in his slippers, feeling bored. No chair, however comfortable, gave him any sense of repose or well-being; his beloved books seemed suddenly devoid of interest now that she was no longer at his side, sewing by the same light he was reading by. And a kind of modesty, a scruple, a vague sense of shame prevented him from going to the theatre.

After her return from Ericeira, he was troubled, too, by a constant unease, knowing that she was only ten minutes away from the house in which he was living alone in that melancholy state of widowerhood. At least twenty times a night, his thoughts made that journey, went up the stairs to Neto's apartment and entered the familiar living room, with its chaise longue upholstered in scarlet cretonne. It was there that she usually sat when they went to visit her Papa; and he felt a pang of jealousy and despair to think of her quietly sitting there, her sewing in her lap or a book in her hand, and not even thinking of him.

Neto had come to see him when they returned from Ericeira. And every word the rascal spoke was like a stab in the heart. They'd had a wonderful time in Ericeira, apparently, although they hadn't really seen anyone socially, Ludovina's circumstances not really allowing for parties or picnics; however, they had enjoyed themselves greatly *en famille*. Ludovina had taken a few sea baths and was looking healthy and plump; indeed, he had never seen her looking quite so well. She had practised the piano a great deal and seemed resigned and, generally speaking, on good form. And having painted this appetising portrait of her, he left without asking the question Godofredo so longed to hear: why did they not make their peace?

He desired this passionately, but, out of a sense of pride and dignity, as well as a remnant of pique and jealousy, he did not want to be the one to make the first move. He felt that Neto should be the person to bring about this reconciliation, and realising why he wanted to keep his daughter at home, he began to hate him. The scoundrel was enjoying her regular monthly allowance of thirty *mil réis*. Godofredo briefly considered withdrawing the allowance, but was deterred from doing so by a sense of chivalry.

What tormented him was the fact that he had not yet seen her. In vain did he repeatedly walk past Neto's house; in vain did he go to Sunday mass, to her church; in vain did he pass by her dressmaker's, Dona Justina's in Largo do Carmo, in the hope of seeing her leave or enter. He did not see her until two days before Christmas. That morning, he was in a tobacconist's shop at the top of the Chiado, when he turned and caught a glimpse of her from behind. He was so shaken that, instead of running after her in order to see her properly, as his desire so angrily demanded, he shrank back into the shop and stood there, hesitating, his heart pounding, looking pale and stupid. Then suddenly, he was filled by a desperate need to see her, but despite walking up and down the Chiado, he could not find her again; he had lost her and went home filled with a terrible longing, and all night he imagined over and over that tall figure, all in black, a yellow flower in her hat.

A week later, however, he was walking along Calçada do Correio, when he spotted her coming from the opposite direction, with her sister. At first, he was just as troubled and embarrassed as on that first occasion, and felt the same urge to hide in a doorway. At last, though, heart thumping, he decided to face the music, and so he drew himself up and marched towards her. Still trembling, he saw out of the corner of his eye how she lowered her eyes and blushed, just as troubled as he was by the encounter.

He returned home in an extraordinary state of exaltation. He adored her, and his heart swooned at the delicious idea of once more holding her in his arms. At the same time, he was filled by furious, diffuse feelings of jealousy: he was jealous of other men, of the street, of the steps she took, of the words she might say to those other men and the way she might look at them. He wanted her all to himself, locked up and safe between his walls, in the prison of his embrace.

He could not bear to stay indoors and, when it was almost midnight, he went out to gaze up at the windows of her father's apartment. He returned home and wrote her an absurd letter, six pages of mingled passion and complaint. When he re-read what he had written, he tore the letter up, finding it, at once, too wordy and insufficiently amorous. He did not sleep that night. He kept seeing her lovely blushing face, her lowered lids. She was, as Neto had said, plumper and more beautiful. She was divine! And she was *his*, *his* wife! His miserable, solitary life could not possibly continue as it was!

January passed without their meeting again, and his passion for her continued to grow. He waited for some chance encounter to bring them together; each morning, he woke thinking that the day could not end without him seeing her, and this time he would speak to her. When he met Neto on another occasion, he had made vague mention of the inconvenience of their continued separation, but Neto had merely given a sad, melancholy, fatherly shrug. Yes, it was all very sad, but what could they do? One night, in Café Martinho, Godofredo spoke to him again. And Neto announced that he had decided to make a little trip to the Minho with his daughter – to avoid any gossip. Godofredo was so taken aback that he could not help but say gruffly:

'Not at my expense, I hope!'

And then he had angrily turned on his heel and stalked off home. It was seven o'clock in the evening and there was a cold, bright moon shining. He had almost reached his front door when he came face to face with Ludovina and her sister. Ludovina drew back, and he, instinctively, stepped off the pavement and was about to walk away; instead, on an impulse, he immediately turned round and hurried towards her, calling:

'Ludovina!'

She, too, had stopped and turned round, looking terrified. They were standing outside a grocery store beneath a gas light, staring at each other, unable to think of a single thing to say, both of them utterly perplexed, their faces bright red. Godofredo was in such a state that he didn't even greet his sister-in-law, indeed, he hadn't even noticed her. His first words were quite absurd:

'I understand you're going to the Minho.'

Ludovina stared at him, astonished, then glanced at her sister.

'To the Minho?' she murmured.

And he stammered out:

'Y-yes, your father told me... I thought it was quite ridiculous. Oh, Teresinha, forgive me, I didn't see you there. How have you been? And you, Ludovina, how have you been?'

Ludovina shrugged:

'Not too bad...'

He couldn't take his eyes off her, and thought she looked utterly adorable in a velvet cloak he hadn't seen before, and which must have been new.

'I hear you had a good time in Ericeira.'

She gave a bitter laugh:

'A good time?' Then added with a sigh: 'Only if you call being bored and crying a lot a good time.'

Godofredo was filled with immense love and pity, and in a tremulous voice, almost crying himself, he said:

'There now...'

Then he added in a familiar tone, as if the reconciliation were complete:

'Things at home haven't been going well either. Margarida has grown very slovenly. And there was something I wanted to ask you. How on earth does one light that reading lamp? I've tried everything.'

She laughed, and so did Teresa. Realising that, from that moment on, she was once more Godofredo's wife, Ludovina said:

'If you like, I can come and show Margarida what to do.'

He almost gave a whoop of joy:

'Yes, come, come! Teresa, you come too. It'll only take a moment.'

He raced up the stairs ahead of them and opened the door, almost swooning with voluptuous delight to hear the rustle of skirts behind him. Hearing voices, Margarida had run to meet him and was flabbergasted when she saw the two ladies. Godofredo was shouting wildly:

'Bring me that reading lamp!'

Ludovina and her sister had gone into the dining room and remained standing, their hats on and their hands modestly clasped before them. Godofredo, meanwhile, had rushed like a mad thing first into the kitchen, then into the bedroom, and then to light the candles in the parlour, where there was no gas. Ludovina was looking around the dining room, shocked at the general air of neglect, noticing with indignation a lovely cut-glass fruit bowl with one handle broken.

Godofredo saw her looking and said:

'You can't imagine how bad things have been. Look, come in here, come and see our bedroom.'

He went ahead, and she blushed as deeply as a virgin entering the nuptial chamber. As soon as they were inside, he grabbed her and dragged her over to the washroom, where, in the darkness, he violently, frenetically kissed her eyes, her hair, her hat, unable to get enough of her soft skin or the coolness she had brought in with her from the cold street.

She said softly:

'Stop! Teresa might see us!'

'Send her away! I'll take her home, if you like,' he murmured. 'But you stay here, my love, and let us never ever part again.'

She consented with a kiss.

IX

The following day, in a moment of tenderness and wanting a more poetic setting for his happiness – and since the weather was gorgeous – Godofredo suggested that they go and spend a few days in Sintra. It was like a second honeymoon. They stayed at the Hotel Lawrence, where they had a small suite all to themselves; they rose late, Godofredo ordered champagne with dinner, and whenever they were alone, walking beneath the trees, he would bestow passionate kisses on her. He did not leave her side for a moment, eager to enjoy their old intimacy, which he had thought lost for ever, taking infinite pleasure in finding her dressing gown draped over a chair or in watching her buttoning up her bodice or combing her hair.

After four days, they returned, but in Lisbon, the honeymoon continued with no expense spared; he even hired a carriage and a box at the Teatro São Carlos. Godofredo wanted to be seen with her everywhere, to silence any malicious tongues. At the theatre, he always took a box next to the stalls, as if to display his domestic bliss. And since Ludovina, after all those weeks in the fresh air in Ericeira, had returned stronger, plumper and even more magnificent in all her sturdy, blonde beauty, she was a frequent object of interest to the gentlemen in the stalls, and there was always at least one pair of opera glasses trained on her.

'Let them look,' Godofredo said. 'They're amazed to see us together, which is exactly what I want.'

Seated at the front of the box, he tugged at his shirt cuffs and smiled at his Lulu.

On one such night, Meyerbeer's *L'Africaine* was being performed for the first time, and in the middle of the fifth act, Ludovina, who had spent the whole performance tortured by the new shoes she was wearing, asked if they could leave. He agreed at once, even though he was enjoying La Alteroni's heart-breaking trills, which she sang against a backdrop of manchineel trees lit by the tragic light of a full moon. He helped Ludovina on with her cloak and gave her his arm; and while they were waiting in a corner of the foyer for their carriage to arrive, Machado suddenly appeared, cigar in mouth, putting on his overcoat. He obviously hadn't seen them, for he continued to whistle as he strolled nonchalantly across the foyer, buttoning up his coat. Suddenly, though, he spotted them! For a moment, he appeared to hesitate, and stood frozen and pale-faced, his fingers fumbling with a button. Then he recovered and very respectfully doffed his hat. Ludovina gave the briefest of nods, then lowered her eyes and stood there, serious, impassive and motionless, clasping the long blue train of her dress. And Godofredo also hesitated before saying a hearty: 'Good evening, Machado!' Machado fled.

When Godofredo went into the office the next morning, Machado was already at his desk. After their usual abrupt exchange of greetings, Godofredo shuffled some papers, read his correspondence and leafed distractedly through the newspaper, but it was clear that his mind was elsewhere. Suddenly, he leaned back, cracked his knuckles, and asked:

'So what did you think of La Alteroni last night?'

This was the first time he had asked Machado anything unrelated to business matters. Machado stood up rather nervously and said:

'Oh, I really liked her. What about you? She has a good voice, don't you think?'

And as soon as these banal words were spoken, it was as if the floodgates were opened. Godofredo stood up too, and a flow of words, hesitant at first, then more spontaneous, formed a vital stream of sympathy that brought them closer together. They were like friends meeting after a long absence; and each recognised the very things they had always admired in the other. A trivial joke by Machado about the tenor made Godofredo burst out laughing, and Machado found Godofredo's remark about the quality of the violin-playing immensely interesting and made him think again that Godofredo was a real connoisseur of music. Then Godofredo told him about their stay in Sintra, and for a while, they chatted about that, each naming his favourite places and describing the impression these had made on them, as if, after their long separation, they felt the need to compare ideas and tastes. Then Machado had to go out, but the farewell handshake they exchanged was deeply felt, a sign of their complete reconciliation, binding them to each other once more and for ever.

Godofredo's life was again serene and happy. Order and joy were restored to the house in Rua de São Bento: his boiled eggs were no longer served raw or over-cooked; at night the *Souvenir d'Andalousie* thrilled him with vague thoughts of the gardens of Granada; and at every moment, the sound of her voice and the rustle of her skirts bathed his heart in happiness. Winter passed and spring came, and the first warm days of March had just arrived when, one morning as he was walking down the corridor on his way out, he happened to glance through a half-open door and see Margarida surreptitiously slipping her mistress a letter. His chest felt as if it had been crushed by a rock. He could barely find the handle on the front door; he immediately imagined another man, another lover, and his happiness, so laboriously rebuilt, cracked in two. He was filled with horror, as if he were the victim of some cruel and bestial fate: the inevitable promiscuity of the female. He was sure it was Machado again, and a wave of blood passed before his eyes; this time, he thought, there would be no discussions, no consultations, no seconds; he would simply walk into the office and put a bullet through Machado's heart at point-blank range.

Such was his agitation that he felt sure he could not bear the sight of Machado. Instead of going to the office, he wandered around the Baixa, unable to rid his mind of the image of the maid's hand, the white piece of paper, Ludovina's embarrassed air. He returned home, sombre and silent. Incapable of sitting still, he roamed from one room to another, slamming doors, like a man in danger of suffocating, feeling the air all around him heavy with deceit and treachery. Ludovina was so alarmed that, in the end, she asked him what was wrong.

'Nerves,' he said brusquely.

And shortly afterwards, giving in to a furious impulse, he turned on her, declaring that he'd had enough of mysteries, that he could not continue to live in that inferno of doubt, and demanding to know what was on the piece of paper that Margarida had given her.

Shocked by such violence, by his strident tone of voice, she stared at him and instinctively placed one hand on the pocket of her dressing gown.

He noticed that gesture and cried:

'Ah, so that's where you put it. Let me see!'

She said she found his distrust offensive. Was he starting all over again with his suspicions and his questions? Could she not receive a letter without him wanting to know what it was?

Deathly pale, fists clenched, he shouted:

'Give me that letter or I'll hit you!'

She turned equally pale, called him rude and cruel, and fell onto the sofa, weeping, her hands covering her face.

'Give me the letter!' he screamed, on tiptoe now. 'Give me the letter! And it won't be like last time, you know. I'll send you straight to a convent. I'll kill you!'

Not even waiting for a response, he launched himself at her, twisting her arm and tearing the pocket of her dressing gown in order to get at the letter. But when he did, he could barely read the writing; it was an illiterate scrawl on a scrap of lined paper. It began 'My dear lady' and was signed 'Maria do Carmo' and spoke of the money given to her, of her little boy now recovered from measles, and of the thankful prayers she would offer up for such a generous gift.

Shaken, shrunken, humiliated, still grasping the paper, he sat down next to Ludovina, who was now sobbing, her face in her hands. Putting his arm about her waist, he stammered:

'It's all right. Forgive me. I see now that it was nothing, but tell me what it's about.'

She pushed him away and stood up, offended. Was he satisfied now? He'd read the letter, hadn't he? And was it from a man, was it?

Profoundly ashamed, he could say only:

'But why all the mystery?'

Seeing her there, so beautiful, wiping away her tears and trying to master her sobs, he could not contain himself; he must have her forgiveness, and so he knelt before her, his hands pressed together as if in prayer, and murmured:

'Forgive me, Lulu, I was a fool…'

Uttering a still louder sob, she slapped him across the face.

And then he almost cried too; he kissed her hands, embraced her knees, then, clinging to her skirts, scrambled to his feet, and covered her neck and throat in kisses. And even while they were embracing, she was telling him the story of the secret gifts of money she had been sending to a young girl she had met in Ericeira, who had been seduced by a scoundrel and then abandoned by him along with their two children, one of whom was not yet weaned.

'But why did you make such a mystery of it, my love?' he asked passionately, touched by her story.

Then she admitted that she had already given the girl more than five *mil réis* and was afraid he might think her extravagant.

And so intense was his joy that he exclaimed:

'What do you mean "extravagant"? Give her another five – from me!'

And it all ended in a kiss.

Godofredo then felt ashamed of his rage that morning against Machado. To think that he had again considered killing Machado! Filled now by great feelings of friendship for him and a vague sense of gratitude, he felt an urgent need to see him and shake him by the hand.

The next day, when he returned to the office, he could not hold back and, for no reason, he embraced Machado. And Machado returned his embrace, apparently unsurprised by such effusive behaviour and with a sad abandon that Alves had not expected. Even more unexpected was the sight of

Machado's eyes, which were red from crying.

'My mother is seriously ill,' Machado said in answer to Godofredo's question.

And Alves, his own joy cut short by his friend's sad news, could only murmur:

'Oh, what dreadful news!'

And it *was* dreadful! The doctor said there was no hope. The poor lady was suffering from a complicated series of ailments affecting liver, bladder and heart, and all these seemed about to come together and undo her life completely. The previous evening, she had passed out and remained unconscious for two hours. Machado had thought she was dead, but she had been so much better this morning, it was quite extraordinary, not that he thought it would last. Poor Machado sighed when he said this. His relationship with his mother had, up until then, been his strongest bond; they had always lived together; indeed, she was the reason he had never wanted to marry, and now that imminent loss seemed about to deprive his life of all that made it dear to him.

'God will intervene,' murmured Godofredo.

Machado shrugged, and moments later, he left the office to return to the bedside of his poor ailing mother.

After that, Godofredo went to Machado's house for news three or even four times a day. The poor lady was sinking fast; fortunately, though, she was in no pain, and her final moments were consoled by the love of her son, who never left her side, concealing his own grief and distress, cheering her up with plans for the future and trips to the country, and joking with her as he had in the good times. Then, one afternoon, when Godofredo went to ask for news, the maid opened the door, wiping her tears away with her apron. Her mistress had died only an hour before, like a little bird. He went in, and Machado fell into his arms, sobbing.

Godofredo did not leave him then. He spent that night there and took care of all the arrangements for the funeral, the invitations, and the purchase of a plot in Alto de São João. The next day, when friends called to offer their condolences, they shook his hand in the same silent, heartfelt way as they did Machado's, recognising in him not so much a brother to Machado as a father.

Many people came to the funeral; there were twenty carriages in all. Godofredo carried the key to the coffin and organised everything, inviting Machado's closest friends to be pall-bearers, talking to the priests, and to everyone else. When the coffin was lowered into the grave, he was the only one who cried.

The following day, Machado left for Vila Franca to stay with an aunt, and Godofredo took him to the station, helped him with his luggage and again wept when they embraced.

A fortnight later, Machado returned and resumed his place at his desk in the office. He was quite changed. He seemed calmer, but so deep in grief that Godofredo, ever the romantic, thought to himself that those lips would never smile again.

Noticing that Machado tended to stay on at the office, unwilling to go home to his now empty house and his solitary supper, Godofredo succumbed to one of his sudden kindly impulses, putting their past history behind them and opening his arms to Machado:

'Look, what's done is done! Come and have dinner with us!'

He didn't even give Machado time to consider, but helped him on with his overcoat, dragged him down the stairs, called a cab, bundled him inside and carried him in triumph to Rua de São Bento. Trembling and already pale with anticipation at the prospect of that meeting, Machado said nothing during the whole journey, desperately trying to think of something natural to say to 'her'. On the stairs, they could hear the sound of the piano, and moments later, Godofredo was sticking his head round the door curtain and exclaiming radiantly:

'Ludovina, I've brought you a visitor!'

She stood up and found herself face to face with Machado, who bowed deeply, hiding his embarrassment in the depth of that bow. She blushed bright scarlet, but her voice remained clear and firm when she held out her hand to him, saying:

'How are you, Senhor Machado? Did you have a good journey?'

He managed to stammer some words of reply and remained standing, slowly rubbing his hands, while Ludovina did her best to dispel any embarrassment by chattering brightly and nervously to Godofredo about a visit she had received from the Mendonças, telling him all about Senhora Mendonça and Mendonça Junior, her ears burning.

Then she left the room to give orders to the maids.

When they were alone, Godofredo remarked sagely:

'As long as people are well brought up, there'll always be a happy ending!'

She returned shortly afterwards, looking calmer, doubtless having applied a little powder to her face. Machado had sat down on the famous yellow sofa, but he sprang up to offer her his place. She declined and sat down on a yellow armchair next to the sofa, and then, as if suddenly remembering a message she had forgotten to give, she blurted out:

'I was so terribly sorry to hear of your loss, Senhor Machado…'

He bowed and murmured a response.

Godofredo exclaimed:

'Oh, let's not talk about that now! One must accept God's decrees, and that's all there is to it.'

However, a shadow passed over Machado's grieving face, and an air of sadness weighed on the room. And it was his sadness that put them all, suddenly, at their ease. It was as if that grieving Machado dressed in full mourning, still fresh from his mother's graveside, was not the same one who had drunk glasses of port wine and held her in his arms on that yellow sofa, but a different Machado, a serious young man in need of consolation, a Machado who had grown older and would be for ever incompatible in their minds with affairs of the heart. She found him greatly altered, and could not now remember what he had been like before; he, too, found her as unfamiliar as if this were the first time he had visited the house. The husband had forgotten, and so had they. They ended by looking at and speaking to each other quite naturally, without any sign of awkwardness, with her addressing him as 'Senhor Machado' and he calling her 'Senhora'; never again would they tremble at the sight of each other; they were as cold now as two burned-out embers.

The dinner was a quiet, calm, friendly, almost jolly affair.

And so life flowed on in its usual easy, banal way. Machado's period of mourning for his mother came to an end, and he resumed his theatre-going, took up with a few more Spanish girls, and flirted with certain married ladies. Then, one day, Neto died of apoplexy while on a tram, and Teresa came to live with her sister. Two years later, Machado married a girl called Cantanhede, for whom he conceived a mad, absurd passion, which could not wait, and so courtship, trousseau, marriage licences and wedding all took place within a month.

There was a ball, to which Ludovina wore a beautiful dress, but she danced very little because she was again wearing the wrong shoes and the ones she had on were so painful, she nearly fainted.

After one year, poor Cantanhede died in childbirth, and once again, Machado sobbed in Godofredo's arms; once again, Godofredo received the key of the coffin and silently, solemnly shook hands with family and friends at the wake. This time, however, Ludovina was there to help him, despite her own grief, for she and poor Cantanhede had become inseparable friends. Indeed, Ludovina's grief was almost as great as Machado's.

Then life flowed on again in its usual easy, banal way. Two years later, Machado took up with an actress from the Teatro do Ginásio. And at around the same time, there was an upset in the Alves household, namely, Teresa's marriage – made against the will of both sister and brother-in-law – to a clerk at the customs and excise, an imbecile, a fool, a nincompoop with not a penny to his name, but with whom Teresa had fallen in love because of his golden hair. In the end, they had no option but to let her marry him because her health had begun to decline, and she swore, among other things, that she would throw herself out of the window.

And the months passed, and then the years. Alves & Co. grew and prospered. The office, now larger and more lavish, employed six clerks and was located on the corner of Rua da Prata. Godofredo had grown balder and Ludovina plumper; they had their own carriage and spent the summers in Sintra. Then Machado married again, this time a widow, an inexplicable choice really because she was neither pretty nor rich, but she had extraordinary dark, voluptuous, thick-lashed eyes that were filled with a kind of swooning languor.

They had a modest wedding and honeymooned in Paris. On their return, they came to live close to Godofredo and Ludovina, who had now moved to a very grand house in Rua de Buenos Aires. And another great friendship immediately sprang up between Ludovina and the lady with the languorous eyes. Ludovina quickly became the slave of that curious creature, who had already enslaved Machado and held absolute sway over Godofredo; indeed, although possessed of no particularly superior qualities, apart from her chubby little self and her thick-lashed, swooningly languorous eyes, she effortlessly dominated everyone around her, servants, acquaintances, even suppliers. The two families live next door to each other now, and are growing old together. There is always a great ball on Ludovina's birthday, a day inseparable in Alves' mind from that other anniversary, their wedding anniversary, when he had arrived home and found her on the yellow sofa. But that was so long ago that the memory now makes him smile and gives him pause for thought as well, for that event remains the major event of his life and from it he draws all his philosophy. As he often says to Machado: 'What a prudent thing prudence is!' If, on the day of the yellow sofa, he had abandoned himself to his jealous rage or had persisted with his ideas of vengeance and rancour, what would his life have been like? He would be living apart from his wife, he would have broken off his personal and commercial relationship with his business partner; his firm would not have prospered nor his fortune increased; and he would have become an embittered old bachelor, under the thumb of his servants, his health perhaps spoiled by licentious living. During those twenty years, how many lovely things he would have missed, how much domestic bliss, how much comfort, how many sweet evenings spent with his family, how many pleasant hours with his friend, how many long days of peace and honour! Instead, he would be a sour, old man, his life and health ruined, and that shameful episode from his past still tormenting him!

What a difference!

He had reached out to his guilty wife and to his faithless friend, and in that simple embrace he had made of her a model wife and of his friend a faithful brother. And there they all were, side by side, honest, contented, rich and happy, growing old together.

Sometimes, when he thinks this, Alves cannot help but smile with satisfaction. Then he claps his friend on the back, reminds him of the past, and says:

'And to think we nearly fought a duel, Machado! Young people are so rash! And over what, friend Machado? Why, nothing at all!'

And Machado, in turn, claps him on the back and answers, smiling:

'Quite right, friend Alves, nothing at all!'

A Lyric Poet

Here, set out in the simplest of terms, without fancy phrases or unnecessary ornament, is the sad story of the poet Korriscosso. Of all the lyric poets I have read or heard about, he, undoubtedly, was the most unfortunate. I met him in London, in the Charing Cross Hotel, in the early hours of a freezing December morning. I had arrived from the Continent, prostrated by the two hours it took to cross the English Channel. What a sea! There was only a fresh northeasterly breeze blowing, but where I lay on deck – beneath the oil-cloth cape with which a sailor had covered me as one might cover a corpse – lashed by the snow and the waves and quailing before the tumultuous darkness, through which the steamboat growled and lurched and battled its way, that breeze felt more like a typhoon from the China Seas.

As soon as I entered the hotel, chilled to the bone and still groggy from lack of sleep, I rushed to the vast fireplace in the foyer, where I gazed reverently at the goodly glow from the coals and basked in the warm peace in which the room lay drowsing. Only then did I notice the long, lean figure in his uniform of white tie and tails, standing on the other side of the fireplace, as silent and sad as a thoughtful stork, and gazing, like me, into the burning coals, a napkin over his arm. But, at that point, the porter had brought in my luggage, and I went to register my name at the desk. The prim, blonde woman in charge, who had the kind of antique profile one might find on a very worn medal, set her crochetwork down beside her cup of tea, gently smoothed her hair and then – with little finger cocked and diamond ring glittering – correctly recorded my name in the book. It was only when I was about to ascend the stately staircase that the thin, tragic figure made a low angular bow and murmured, clearly enunciating every syllable:

'Seven o'clock breakfast is being served, sir.'

But I didn't want the seven o'clock breakfast and instead went up to my room to sleep.

Later, when I came down to the restaurant for lunch, feeling rested and refreshed from my bath, I spotted that same sad, thin figure stationed in melancholy fashion by the large window. The empty room was bathed in a greyish light; the fires in the stoves flickered; and outside, in the Sunday silence, in the dumb streets, the snow was falling ceaselessly from a dull, yellowish sky. I could see only the man's back, but was immediately intrigued by the air of despair emanating from his thin, slightly stooped silhouette. His flowing, shoulder-length locks, worthy of a tenor, were clearly those of a Southern European, and every part of his skinny frame, unaccustomed to the cold, shrank from the sight of those snow-covered roofs and the pale silence outside. I called him over. And when he turned round, I was greatly struck by his face, which I had only glimpsed when I arrived in the early hours; it was a long, sad, very dark face, with a Jewish nose and a short, curly beard, the beard of a Christ in a Romantic painting; his forehead or, rather, as fine literature would, I believe, describe it, his brow, was broad and lustrous. His deep-set eyes were filled with a sweet, fluid, dreamy indecision. And he was so thin! When he walked, his too-short trousers flapped about his shins like a flag about a flagpole; his jacket hung on his body like an ample tunic; the two long, pointed tails of his tailcoat looked quite simply grotesque. He took my order without even looking at me, as if resigned to the tedium of the task; he then slouched over to the counter (where the maître d'hôtel was engrossed in reading the Bible), ran one limp, mournful hand over his hair and said in a flat voice:

'Room number 307. Two cutlets. Tea...'

The maître d'hôtel put down his Bible and made a note of the order, while I settled myself at my table and opened the edition of Tennyson I had brought with me for company over lunch, because, as I believe I mentioned, it was Sunday, a day devoid of newspapers and fresh bread. Outside, snow continued to fall on the silent city. At a distant table, an old gentleman with a brick-red complexion, white hair and sidewhiskers had finished his lunch and was dozing, hands resting on his belly, mouth open and spectacles poised on the end of his nose. And the only sound from the street was the mournful voice, further muffled by the snow, of a beggar on the opposite corner intoning a psalm. A typical Sunday in London.

The thin waiter brought me my lunch, and as soon as he approached, bearing the tea tray, I sensed at once that he was both interested in and impressed by the book of Tennyson's poems I was holding. I knew this from the rapid, greedy glance he gave the open pages, the almost imperceptible tremor that ran through him, a very fleeting emotion, it's true, for, having set down the tea things, he turned on his heel and resumed his melancholy pose by the window, his sad gaze fixed on the equally sad snow outside. I attributed his curiosity to the book's splendid binding, an edition of *The Idylls of the King* in black Morocco leather, with the coat of arms of Lancelot of the Lake on the front – a golden pelican above a green sea.

I left that night on the express train for Scotland, and even before I had passed drowsy, grave, episcopal York, I had already forgotten all about the romantic figure of that waiter at the Charing Cross Hotel. It was not until a month later, on my return to London, that I felt my initial interest rekindle when I entered the restaurant and saw again that slow, fateful figure crossing the room carrying a plate of roast beef in one hand and, in the other, a dish of mashed potatoes. And that night, I experienced the singular joy of discovering his name and glimpsing a fragment of his past life. It was late, and I was just walking back from Covent Garden, when I encountered in the hotel foyer my majestic, prosperous friend, Bracolletti.

You don't know Bracolletti? He is a formidable presence, possessing, as he does, the paunchy amplitude, the thick black beard, and the ceremonious slowness of a plump pasha; however, this ponderous Turkish gravity is tempered in Bracolletti by his smile and his eyes. What eyes he has! The same sweet, tender eyes I have seen in the beasts of Syria. There seems to hover in that soft, liquid gaze the gentle religiosity of those races who have given us our Messiahs. And that smile! Bracolletti's smile is complex and perfect, the richest of all human expressions; in those lips that open to reveal the brilliant white teeth of a virgin, there is refinement, innocence, bonhomie, surrender, the gentlest of ironies, and persuasion! His smile is Bracolletti's fortune.

Bracolletti is a very shrewd fellow. He was born in Smyrna of Greek parents, but that is all he will reveal; otherwise, if you ask him about his past, the good Greek tilts his head from side to side, charmingly closes his Mohammedan eyes, unleashes a smile so sweet it could tempt bees, and murmurs, as if drowning in kindness and pity:

'*Eh! Mon Dieu! Eh! Mon Dieu!*'

And that's all. He is obviously much-travelled, though, because he knows Peru, the Crimea, the Cape of Good Hope, and other such exotic places, as intimately as he knows Regent Street, and it is clear to everyone that his life has not been that of the usual vulgar adventurer from the Levant, a combination of gold and oakum, splendour and rags; he is a plump man and, therefore, prudent; a magnificent solitaire diamond ring glitters on his hand; in a cold snap, he always has an opulent fur coat to put on; and every week, at the Fraternal Club, of which he is a much-loved member, he wins at least ten pounds at whist. He really is a sterling chap.

He has one weakness – a penchant for young girls of between twelve and fourteen; he likes them thin and fair and foul-mouthed. He methodically picks them up from the poorest areas of London and installs them in his home, like birds in a cage; he feeds them gruel and dotingly listens to their chatter; he encourages them to steal shillings from his pockets and leaves bottles of gin within easy reach so that he can gloatingly observe the growth of vice in those flowers of the London mud; and when one of them, hair all dishevelled and face ablaze, insults him, attacks him and babbles obscenities, good Bracolletti, sitting cross-legged on the sofa, his hands beatifically folded over his belly, eyes ecstatic, murmurs in his Syrian Italian:

'*Piccolina! Gentilleta!*'

Dear old Bracolletti! It was with genuine pleasure that I embraced him that night in Charing Cross, and since we hadn't seen each other for a long time, we decided to dine together in the hotel restaurant. There was the same sad waiter standing at the counter, bent over a copy of the *Journal des Débats*. And as soon as he saw Bracolletti in all his rotund majesty, he silently held out his hand to him, and they exchanged solemn, tender, sincere greetings.

Good heavens, the two men were friends! But like the gods of Attica, who withdrew to the safety of their cloud-home whenever they got into trouble on Earth, Bracolletti took refuge in his usual:

'*Eh! mon Dieu! Eh! mon Dieu!*'

'Come on, Bracolletti! I want to know his story. There must be a story behind that fateful, Byronic face…'

Bracolletti then did his best to look as innocent as his paunch and beard would allow, and admitted – feeding me one short sentence at a time – that they had travelled together in Bulgaria and in Montenegro… Korriscosso had been his secretary. Beautiful handwriting… Difficult times… *Eh! mon Dieu!*…

'Where is he from?'

Bracolletti responded without hesitation, lowering his voice and making a disdainful gesture.

'He's a Greek from Athens.'

My interest vanished like water in sand. When one has travelled in the Orient and visited the Levantine ports, one soon acquires the habit of distrusting Greeks. At first, especially if one is university-educated and versed in the classics, one waxes enthusiastic and thinks of Alcibiades and Plato, the glories of a free, aesthetic race, and one conjures up the august outlines of the Parthenon. However, once you have got to know them a little, at the tables and on the quarterdecks of the ships of the Messageries Maritimes, and especially after hearing accounts of the trail of skulduggery they have left behind them all the way from Smyrna to Tunis, any other Greek you come across provokes one of three responses: quickly buttoning up your jacket; crossing your arms over your watch chain; and sharpening your wits so as to not to be caught out by some swindle. This dire reputation stems from the fact that the only Greeks who travel to the ports of the Levant are a vile breed, part-pirate, part-lackey, like clever, evil birds of prey. Indeed, as soon as I learned that Korriscosso was Greek, I immediately remembered how, on my last stay at the hotel, my beautiful edition of Tennyson had vanished from my room and I recalled, too, the look of plundering greed with which Korriscosso had eyed it. The man was a thief.

And during the meal, we spoke no more of Korriscosso. We were served by another waiter, fresh-faced, honest and healthy. The lugubrious Korriscosso did not leave his counter, immersed in reading the *Journal des Débats*.

When I went to my room that night, I got lost. The hotel was packed, and I had been lodged on one of the upper floors, in a labyrinth of corridors, stairs, corners and angles, where one almost needed a map and compass.

Candlestick in hand, I plunged down a corridor that had the warm, stuffy feel of a narrow alleyway. The doors there had no numbers, only small cards bearing names: John, Smith, Charlie, Willie… These were obviously the servants' quarters. One door stood open and from it came the glow of a gas lamp. I walked towards the light and saw Korriscosso, still in his tailcoat, sitting writing at a table overflowing with papers, his head resting on his hand.

'Could you tell me the way to room number 508?' I stammered.

He looked at me with vague, startled eyes, as if returning from somewhere very far away, from another universe; he blinked and repeated:

'508? 508?'

That was when I spotted on the table, among papers, grubby collars and a rosary, my edition of Tennyson! The thief saw my look, and the blush that flooded his gaunt cheeks condemned him outright. My first instinct was to ignore the book; however, since this was a kindly instinct, worthy of the superior morality of a Talleyrand, I repressed it and, pointing at the book with one stern finger, the finger of an angry Providence, I said:

'That's my Tennyson!'

I can't remember now what his stammered response was, because, taking pity on him and seized again by the curiosity I felt for the picaresque figure of that sentimental Greek, I added in a voice full of forgiveness and understanding:

'He's a great poet, don't you think? I'm sure you've enjoyed reading him…'

Korriscosso blushed still more deeply, but not out of the humiliated pique of a robber caught red-handed; it was, I thought, pure shame at having his intelligence and his poetic tastes revealed while he was dressed in the worn tailcoat of a waiter. He did not answer, but when I opened the book, the pages answered for him; the broad white margins were filled with closely written comments in pencil: Sublime! Marvellous! Divine! Words scrawled in a feverish, tremulous hand, shaken by a passionate sensibility.

Korriscosso, meanwhile, had remained respectfully, guiltily standing, head bowed, white tie askew. Poor Korriscosso! I felt sorry for him as he stood there in a stance that spoke of a whole luckless past filled with the sadness of dependency. Remembering that nothing so impresses the men of the Levant as the dramatic and theatrical, I reached out both hands to him in a gesture worthy of the great French actor Talma, and said:

'I, too, am a poet!'

Such an extravagant gesture would have seemed grotesque and impudent to a Northerner, but he immediately identified me as a soulmate. Did I mention what Korriscosso was writing on that sheet of paper? It was poetry or, to be more precise, an ode.

Shortly afterwards, with the door closed, Korriscosso recounted his story, or, rather, fragments and scraps of his biography. His is such a sad story that I can only summarise it here. Besides, whole years went unaccounted for, and I cannot, therefore, attempt a logical, sequential version of this sentimental Greek's life. It was all very vague and dubious. He had, in fact, been born in Athens; his father, it seems, was a porter in Piraeus. When he was eighteen, Korriscosso worked as a servant to a doctor and, when he wasn't working, studied at the University of Athens; as he put it, such things are common *là-bas*. He graduated in law, and later on, in difficult times, his studies allowed him to get work as a hotel interpreter. His first elegies, published in a poetry magazine entitled *Echoes from Attica*, dated from that time. This led directly into politics and parliamentary ambitions. A love affair, an emotional crisis, his lover's brutish husband and subsequent death threats forced him to leave the country. He travelled in Bulgaria, and found employment in a branch of the Ottoman Bank in Thessalonika; while there, he submitted mournful threnodies to a provincial newspaper – *The Argolida Trumpet*. There then followed one of the many lacunae or black holes in his story, and he next reappeared in Athens wearing a new suit and working as a liberal member of parliament.

This moment of glory was short-lived, but enough to bring him fame; he delighted Athens with his colourful, poetic speeches, adorned with inventive, glittering images; as he himself said, he had the gift of making the most barren soil bloom; he could evoke Theocritus' idylls even during a debate on taxation or transport. In Athens, talent leads to power; Korriscosso was appointed to run a ministry; alas, the government, along with most of its members, of whom Korriscosso was the star turn, fell, vanished – who knows why – in one of those sudden political breakdowns so common in Greece, where administrations, like the houses in Athens, often do collapse for no other reason than poor foundations and the decrepitude of both materials and individuals. In a land of ruins everything tends to dust.

Another lacuna, another black hole in Korriscosso's story.

He resurfaced as a member of a republican club in Athens and wrote an article in a newspaper, demanding the emancipation of Poland and a Greece governed by a council of geniuses. Later, he published his *Sighs from Thrace*. This was followed by another love affair that obliged him to seek refuge in England, although he gave me no explanation as to why. After trying various employments in London, he had finally found his current position as a waiter in the Charing Cross Hotel.

'It's a port in a storm,' I said, squeezing his hand.

He smiled bitterly. It was indeed a port in a storm, and it had its advantages. He was well fed; he received reasonable tips; he slept on an old sprung mattress – but at every moment, his delicate soul received painful wounds.

That poor lyric poet spent dreadful, tormenting days forced to wait on rich, gluttonous bourgeois customers and serve them cutlets and glasses of beer! It wasn't the servitude that bothered him; his Greek soul wasn't particularly greedy for freedom; it was enough that his employer treated him courteously. And, as he himself told me, the customers at the hotel never asked him for the mustard or the cheese without saying 'Please'; and when they left, they always touched their hats as they passed; this was enough to satisfy Korriscosso's dignity.

No, the real torment was having to be in constant contact with food. If he were a bookkeeper for a banker or chief cashier in a warehouse selling silks and velvets, at least that would have a glimmer of poetry – the buying and selling of millions, the merchant fleets, the brute force of gold, or else

112

showing off fabrics, rolls of silk, shimmering *moirés*, holding up velvets to show how they fell... But in a restaurant, slicing up beef or ham, what possible scope was there for exercising one's taste, one's artistic originality, one's feeling for colour and dramatic effect? Besides, as he said, serving food meant serving the belly, the stomach, the lowest of our material needs; in a restaurant, the belly is God; the soul is left outside, like a hat on a hatstand or a rolled-up newspaper in an overcoat pocket.

And the people one had to mix with! The lack of conversation! They never turned to him except to order some salami or sardines! He never opened his lips – those lips upon which the Athens parliament had once hung – except to ask: 'More bread?' 'More beef?' Being deprived of opportunities to speak was painful to him.

Worse, working as a waiter got in the way of his true vocation. Korriscosso composed sweet, harmonious odes in his head, while he was walking up and down the room, pushing back his long hair. However, the gluttonous interruption of a customer's voice demanding food was fatal to this way of working. Sometimes, while leaning in a window, napkin over his arm, Korriscosso would be busy writing an elegy filled with moonlight, the white robes of pale virgins, celestial horizons, the flowers of a grieving soul... Ah, he was happy then, up there in the poetic heavens, on the blue plains of dreams, galloping from star to star... Then, suddenly, a coarse, hungry voice would call out:

'Beef and potatoes!'

And those winged fantasies would scatter like startled doves! And poor Korriscosso, hurled down from those ideal heights, shoulders drooping, the tails of his tailcoat swaying, would ask with a wan smile:

'Well done or rare?'

Ah, what a bitter fate!

'But,' I asked, 'why don't you leave this place, this temple to the belly?'

He hung his handsome poet's head, and almost weeping in my arms, the knot of his white tie all awry, he told me what kept him there: Korriscosso was in love.

He was in love with Fanny, a maid-of-all-work at the hotel. He had loved her from the very first day he arrived at the hotel; he had fallen in love with her the moment he saw her scrubbing the stone steps, saw her plump, bare arms and her fair hair, her thick coppery, dull gold hair fashioned into a goddess' plait, that fatal blonde hair that so bewitches southerners. And then there was her complexion, which was that of a Yorkshire girl – all milk and roses.

And how Korriscosso had suffered! He poured all his pain into odes, which he wrote out neatly on Sundays, that traditional day of rest and the day of the Lord! He read them to me. And I saw how passion can trouble a sensitive soul; what fiery language, what despair, what lacerating cries were hurled forth from those attic rooms in Charing Cross into the cold, mute sky! Korriscosso, you see, was jealous. That wretch Fanny took no notice of the delicate, sentimental poet by her side and was in love with a policeman! A policeman, a colossus, a Hercules, a mountain of flesh bristling with a forest of beard, with a chest like the side of a battleship and legs like Norman fortresses. This Polyphemus, as Korriscosso called him, was normally on duty in the Strand, and poor Fanny spent her days peering out at him from a window high up in the hotel.

All her savings went on pints of gin and brandy, which she smuggled out to him at night under her apron; she kept him faithful with alcohol. The monster would stand, huge, on the corner, and receive the drink in silence, toss it down his dark gullet, belch loudly, run one hairy hand over his Herculean beard and, without so much as a 'Thank you' or an 'I love you', continue on his way, the vast, sonorous soles of his boots echoing on the pavement. Poor Fanny would gaze adoringly after him. And at that moment, on the other corner, poor, thin Korriscosso would perhaps be standing in the fog like a very weedy telegraph post, weeping and pressing transparent hands to his gaunt face.

Poor Korriscosso! If he could at least touch her heart, but she despised his sad, consumptive body, and did not understand his soul. Not that Fanny was beyond the reach of ardent feelings expressed in melodious language, but Korriscosso could only write his elegies in his mother tongue. And Fanny did not know Greek. And Korriscosso is only a great man – in Greek.

When I went down to my room, I left him sobbing on his bed. I have seen him on other subsequent visits to London. He has grown even thinner, even more doom-laden, more eaten away by jealousy, more bent as he moves about the restaurant carrying the tray of roast beef, more exalted in his lyricism… Whenever he serves me, I give him a shilling tip and, afterwards, on my way out, shake him sincerely by the hand.

At the Mill

In the considered opinion of the whole town Dona Maria da
Piedade was 'a model lady'. Old Nunes the Postmaster would
stroke the few hairs on his otherwise bald head and say:

'She's a saint, that's what she is!'

The town took a kind of pride in her delicate, touching
beauty; she was fair-haired, had a fine profile and ivory skin,
and her sweet, sombre, almost violet-coloured eyes were
shaded by long lashes. She lived at the end of the street in a blue
house with three balconies; and to those who were in the habit
of taking a stroll to the mill, it was always a pleasure to see her
through the window, framed by the thin cotton curtains, bent
over her sewing, always thoughtful and serious and dressed all
in black. She rarely went out. Her husband, who was older and
an invalid, was usually confined to bed because of an illness
affecting his spine; he hadn't left the house for years; frail and
shrunken, he could occasionally be seen at the window too,
leaning on a walking stick, wrapped in his dressing gown, his
face pale and gaunt, his beard untrimmed, and wearing a silk
beret pulled well down on his head. They had three equally
sickly children, two girls and a boy, glum, tearful creatures,
afflicted by boils on their ears. And the house was just as
gloomy. Everyone had to walk on tiptoe because the master of
the house, his nerves on edge because of his insomnia, found
the slightest noise irritating; on the sideboard stood a few
bottles of medicine and a bowl containing linseeds left to soak;
even the flowers with which she adorned the tables – wanting

things to look nice and fresh – soon faded in that stuffy, febrile atmosphere, never aired for fear of draughts; the children were either to be seen with a poultice on one ear or else sitting on a sofa, swathed in blankets, looking sallow and forlorn.

Maria da Piedade's life had been like this since she was twenty. Hers had been a sad existence even when she was single and living with her parents. Her mother was a sour, disagreeable woman, and whenever her father did come home, for he spent most of his time drunk in bars and gambling dens, he sat sullen and silent by the fire, smoking his pipe and spitting into the coals. He beat his wife every week. When João Coutinho asked Maria to marry him, she accepted unhesitatingly, almost gratefully, even though he was already ill, so as to avoid her parents being evicted from the hovel that was their home and so that she would no longer have to hear her mother's screams, which made her tremble and pray upstairs in her bedroom, where the rain came in through the roof. She certainly didn't love her husband, and even in the town, people regretted that Maria's lovely virginal face and exquisite figure should belong to João Coutinho, who had been a cripple since he was a lad. On his father's death, Coutinho had become rich, and once she had grown accustomed to her ill-tempered husband, who spent the day hobbling grimly from living room to bedroom, she might have been resigned to her lot – for she was a natural nurse and consoler – had her children at least been healthy and robust. But she was greatly saddened by the fact that, born as they were with their blood already corrupt, those hesitant lives seemed to rot away in her very hands despite all her anxious care and attention. Sometimes, when she sat alone with her sewing, tears would run down her cheeks and she would be filled by a weariness with life, like a mist darkening her soul.

But if her husband called out to her desperately from within

118

or she heard one of the children sobbing, she would wipe her eyes and go to them, wearing her usual lovely, calm face, to offer a consoling word, to plump up a pillow or to bring good cheer, pleased to be able to offer a little kindness. Her sole ambition was that her own small world should be well treated and well loved. She had never, in all her married life, felt a flicker of curiosity, desire or caprice: her only interest was ensuring that her patients took their medicines at the prescribed times and that they slept well. If she could make them happy, nothing was too much trouble; although not strong herself, she would spend hours holding her youngest child in her arms, for he was the most troublesome, suffering, as he did, from sores that formed a dark crust on his poor little lips; if her husband couldn't sleep, then she would not sleep either, but would sit at the foot of the bed, talking to him or reading out loud from *The Lives of the Saints*, because the poor cripple was extremely devout. In the morning, she might be a touch paler than usual, but still impeccable in her black dress, with her shining hair caught back, having made herself pretty in order to serve the little ones their bread and milk. Her one distraction was to sit by the window in the afternoon with her sewing on her lap while the children played sadly and quietly on the floor. The landscape she could see from there was as monotonous as her life: down below lay the road and, beyond, some bare, rolling fields planted here and there with olive trees and, in the background, a bleak hill without so much as a house, a tree, or even some companionable smoke to add a lively, human note to the dreary solitude of the place.

When some of the other ladies saw how resigned and submissive she was, they declared she was a saint, and yet no one saw her at church, except on Sundays with her oldest child, pale in his blue velvet suit. Indeed, her devotions were restricted to that weekly mass. There was too much to keep her occupied in her own household for her to be overly concerned about Heaven; performing her loving duty as a mother was sufficient satisfaction, and she had no need to adore saints or to be moved by Jesus. She even felt instinctively that any excessive love bestowed on the Lord, any time spent kneeling at the confessional or before the altar, would be a cruel diminution of her role as nurse; her way of praying was to care for her children; and she felt that her poor, increasingly bed-ridden husband, utterly dependent on her, with only her to tend him, had far more right to her fervour than that other man nailed on a cross, with all of humanity to cheer him on. Besides, she had never experienced the kind of sad, sentimental feelings that lead some people to religious devotion. The long habit of running that hospital-cum-home, of being the centre, strength and succour of those poor invalids had made her tender but practical; and that was how she ran the household, with the affectionate good sense and solicitude of a provident mother. These occupations were quite enough to fill her day; besides, her husband hated visitors – all those healthy faces and trite words of commiseration; indeed, months went by during which only family voices were heard, with the exception of Dr Abílio, who adored her and would say, wide-eyed:

'She's an angel! An angel!'

There was, therefore, great excitement in the house when João Coutinho received a letter from his cousin Adrião, announcing his arrival in town in the next two or three weeks. Adrião was famous, and Maria da Piedade's husband was inordinately proud of him. He had even subscribed to a Lisbon newspaper for the sole purpose of being able to see his cousin's name mentioned in articles and reviews. Adrião was a novelist, and his latest book, *Madalena* – a finely crafted study of a woman, full of delicate, subtle analysis – had marked him out as a master. According to his reputation – which, in their small town, had something of the legend about it – he was an interesting fellow, a hero in Lisbon, beloved of noble ladies, impetuous and brilliant, destined for some lofty post in government. In the town, though, he was notable largely for being João Coutinho's cousin.

The prospect of this visit terrified Dona Maria da Piedade. She could already imagine how the presence of this extraordinary guest would create chaos in her house. She would have to take more care over how she dressed, change the time they ate dinner, converse with the literary gentleman and make other painful efforts! The idea of having the sad peace of her hospital invaded by that worldly creature, with his luggage, his cigar smoke, his healthy laughter, seemed, to her horrified sensibilities, almost a profanation. And so she was relieved, even grateful, when Adrião arrived and took up lodgings in Tio André's old inn at the other end of town. João Coutinho, on the other hand, was scandalised: his cousin's room was ready and prepared, complete with lace-trimmed sheets and damask bedspread; the best silver had been set out on the sideboard; and he wanted his cousin – the famous man, the great author – all to himself. Adrião, however, demurred, saying:

'I have my habits, you have yours. We would only get on each other's nerves. But I will dine with you, if I may, each evening. Besides, I'm fine at Tio André's. I have a view from my window over a mill and its pond, which makes for a very pretty picture. And that way we'll stay friends.'

Maria da Piedade gazed at him in amazement, for that hero, that breaker of hearts, that poet glorified in the newspapers, was a very simple fellow, far less complicated and far less ostentatious than the local tax-collector's son! He wasn't even handsome; indeed, with his broad-brimmed hat, his square, bearded face, his light flannel jacket flapping loosely about his small, sturdy body, and his enormous shoes, she thought he resembled one of the local hunters she sometimes saw when she made her monthly visit to the shops on the other side of the river. He didn't use fancy words or phrases either, and the first time he came to dine with them, he spoke cheerily about the business that had brought him there. Of his father's fortune, the only property that had not been sold or mortgaged up to the hilt was Curgossa, an estate near town, which brought in scarcely any rent at all. He wanted to sell it, but this seemed to him as difficult an undertaking as writing *The Iliad*! What a shame his cousin was bedridden and unable to help him in his dealings with the local landowners! It was, then, with great joy that he heard João Coutinho declare that his wife would act as negotiator and would prove as skilled in these matters as any pettifogging lawyer!

'She'll go with you to the estate, talk to Teles and arrange everything. As for the asking price, leave all that to her!'

'What a find you are, cousin!' exclaimed an astonished Adrião. 'An angel who's good with numbers!'

For the first time in her life, Maria da Piedade blushed at a man's compliment. Then she prepared herself to be her cousin's land agent.

The next day, they went to see the property. Since it was quite close and the March day was fresh and bright, they set off on foot. At first, feeling constrained by the company of this literary lion, the poor lady walked beside him like a small, frightened bird; for even though he was the most unpretentious of men, there was something strong and dominating about his energetic, muscular figure, the rich timbre of his voice, and his small, shining eyes, something that perplexed and inhibited her. The hem of her dress got caught on a bramble and when, stooping down, he delicately detached it, the contact of that fine, white, artist's hand on the hem of her skirt troubled her strangely. She hurried on so as to reach the property as quickly as possible, arrive at an agreement with Teles and return at once to take refuge, as if in her natural element, in the sad, stifling air of her hospital. However, the road stretched ahead of them, long and white, beneath the warm sun, and Adrião's words slowly accustomed her to his presence.

He seemed distressed by the sadness of her house and gave her some good advice: the children needed fresh air, sun, something other than that bedroom stuffiness.

She agreed, but explained that whenever she mentioned going to spend some time at their house in the country, poor João would get into a terrible state: he had a horror of fresh air and wide open spaces; raw nature almost made him faint; he had become an entirely artificial being, cloistered behind the curtains around his bed.

He commiserated with her. There must, of course, be a certain satisfaction in a duty so devoutly fulfilled, but she must, nevertheless, have moments when she longed for something else beyond those four walls impregnated with the breath of invalids.

'What else could I want?' she asked.

Adrião did not answer. He had not meant that she might long to see Lisbon or visit the theatre – that would be absurd. He had in mind quite different appetites, the ambitions of a dissatisfied heart, but this seemed too grave and delicate a matter to speak of to such a serious, virginal creature; he spoke instead about the landscape.

'Have you visited the mill?' she asked.

'I would love to if you'd care to take me, cousin.'

'It's too late today.'

However, they agreed to visit that green haven, the town's most idyllic spot, on another occasion.

When they reached the property to be sold, the ensuing long conversation with Teles brought Adrião and Maria da Piedade much closer. The sale, which she negotiated with all the guile of a peasant woman, gave them a common interest. On the way back, she was less reserved, for there was a touching respect in his manner that drew her out despite herself and caused her to confide her innermost thoughts to him; she had never talked so much to anyone; she had certainly never allowed someone else even a glimpse of the constant, hidden melancholy that filled her soul. Otherwise, her complaints returned always to the same griefs – her inner sadness, the illnesses, the endless anxieties... She felt a great sympathy for him, a vague desire to have him always with her, now that he had become the repository of her woes.

Adrião returned to his room at the inn, feeling moved and intrigued by that sad, gentle creature. She was utterly different from the women he had known until then; meeting her was like coming across the sweet profile of a gothic angel among the gargoyles. Everything about her fitted so perfectly; the gold of her hair, the softness of her voice, her modest melancholy, her chaste appearance, all combined to make of her a delicate, touching creature, a creature made still more charming by her petit-bourgeois mind, her vaguely peasant roots, and even a slight commonness; she was an angel who had lived for a long time in a coarse little town, imprisoned by the many trivialities of the place, but the merest breath could make her rise up to the heavens, to the pure summits of romantic love.

He found it both absurd and despicable to pay court to his cousin's wife, but despite himself, he began pondering the delicious pleasure of making an as-yet-uncorseted heart beat faster and of finally placing his lips on a cheek bare of powder. What tempted him further was the thought that he could travel the whole of Portugal and never find a similarly graceful figure so imbued with the touching purity of a sleeping soul. Such an opportunity would not return.

Their walk to the mill proved delightful. It was a little corner of nature worthy of Corot, especially at that noonday hour, when it was all green and cool in the shade of the great trees and among the multifarious murmurings of the flowing water that ran, singing and glittering, over the moss and stones, carrying with it, and scattering all around, the fresh leafy air. The mill was very picturesque with its old tower built of ancient stones, its huge wheel, almost rotten and overgrown with weeds, stationary above the dark, icy, limpid water. Adrião thought it worthy of a scene in a novel, or rather, as the dwelling-place of a nymph. Maria da Piedade said nothing, finding it extraordinary that he should so admire Tio Costa's old, abandoned mill. She was a little weary, and so they sat down on the uneven stone stairs, whose final steps were submerged in the waters of the mill pond; and there they sat in silence for a moment, in that delicious, murmurous coolness, listening to the birds singing in the trees. Adrião studied her out of the corner of his eye; she was slightly bent over, digging out the weeds that grew among the steps with the tip of her sunshade; she looked utterly lovely like that, so pale, so fair, silhouetted against the blue background of the sky; her hat was in bad taste and she was wearing a rather antiquated cape, but even in that he found a kind of piquant innocence. Islanded by the silence of the fields, he began, almost without thinking, to speak to her in a low voice. At first, he spoke again of his pity for her melancholy existence in that gloomy town, for her fate as the eternal nurse. She listened, eyes lowered, amazed and fearful to find herself so alone with that strong, healthy man, and delighting in her fear. At one point, he said how he would love to stay for ever in the town.

'Stay here? But why?' she asked, smiling.

'Why? So as to be always near you.'

She blushed furiously and dropped her sunshade. Adrião was afraid he had offended her and immediately added with a laugh:

'Wouldn't that be nice? I could rent this mill and become a miller. You could be my first customer.'

That made her laugh. She was even prettier when she laughed: everything about her glowed – her teeth, her skin, the colour of her hair. He expanded his joke about becoming a miller by imagining himself travelling the roads with a donkey laden with sacks of flour.

'And I'll come and help you, cousin!' she said, emboldened by her own laughter and by the good humour of the man beside her.

'Yes, do!' he cried. 'I really will become a miller then! What a paradise, eh? The two of us living together at the mill, happily earning our living and listening to the blackbirds singing.'

She blushed again at the fervent tone in which he spoke and drew back as if he were actually about to drag her bodily into the mill. Greatly taken with his own idea, Adrião was now painting her a word picture of a romantic life of idyllic happiness in that green hideaway. Up early each morning to work; then, dining al fresco at the water's edge; and, at night, sitting talking by the light of the stars or beneath the warm shelter of dark summer skies…

And suddenly, he took her in his arms and kissed her on the lips, a long, profound kiss. She did not resist, but lay against his chest, looking pale as death. Two tears ran down her cheeks. She looked so sad, so frail that he released her; she sprang to her feet, picked up her sunshade and stood before him, her lower lip trembling, and murmured:

'That was wrong… that was very wrong…'

He himself was so troubled that he let her go back down to the path alone, but, shortly afterwards, they were again walking silently along together to the town. It was only when he reached the inn that he thought: 'What a fool I am!'

Deep down, though, he was pleased with his own generosity. That night he went to her house and there she was with the youngest child on her lap; she was washing the sores on the child's leg with rose-mallow water. It now seemed to him loathsome to take that woman away from her patients. Besides, that moment at the mill would not return. It would be absurd to stay there in that hateful provincial town, coolly corrupting such an excellent mother. The following day – having concluded the sale of his father's property – he came in the afternoon to say goodbye; he was leaving that evening on the coach. He found her in the living room, seated, as usual, by the window, with her ailing offspring huddled around her. She heard the news of his departure without changing colour, without a sigh, but Adrião noticed that her hand was cold as marble, and when he left, Maria da Piedade remained with her face turned towards the window, looking abstractedly out at the darkening landscape, so that her children would not see the tears falling onto her sewing.

She loved him. From the very first day, his strong, resolute body, his shining eyes, his very manliness had gripped her imagination. What fascinated her about him was not his talent, his reputation in Lisbon, nor the women he had loved; that all seemed to her vague and barely comprehensible; no, what bewitched her was his seriousness, his sane, honest air, his robust good health, his grave, rich voice. She could see other possible lives beyond that life spent bound to an invalid, lives that did not consist of always having before one's eyes a weak, moribund face nor of spending every night waiting for the various times at which to dole out medicine. He was like a blast of air impregnated with all the living force of nature sweeping suddenly through her stuffy room, an air she had breathed deliciously in. Then there had been those conversations in which he had shown himself to be so kind, serious and sensitive; and added to his physical strength, which she greatly admired, was a strong, manly, tender heart to captivate her. This latent love overwhelmed her one night when this idea, this vision came to her: 'What if *he* were my husband!" A shudder ran through her and she desperately clasped her arms about her own body as if confusing herself with her image of him, and trying to clasp that image to her, seeking refuge in its strength. And then, at the mill, he had kissed her. And now he had left!

There began for Maria da Piedade a life as the abandoned woman. Suddenly, everything about her – her husband's illness, her children's ailments, her sad, monotonous days, her sewing – all seemed to her dreary and dull. Now that she did not pour her soul into her duties, they felt as heavy as unfair burdens. She saw her existence as a terrible tragedy, and, although she did not yet rebel, she suffered terrible feelings of exhaustion, when every part of her being felt weary, when she would slump down in a chair, her arms hanging loose, and murmur:

'When will this end?'

She took refuge in her love as a delicious reward. Believing it to be entirely pure, entirely spiritual, she allowed that love slowly to penetrate her soul. In her imagination, Adrião had become a creature of extraordinary qualities; he was all that was strong and beautiful; he was a reason to live. She wanted to know everything about him, everything that came from him. She read all his books, especially *Madalena*, a woman who had loved and died alone. These readings soothed her and provided a kind of solace for her desire. Weeping over the sorrows of those literary heroines seemed to bring relief from her own griefs.

This need to fill her imagination with love affairs and tragic dramas gradually took her over. For months she did nothing but devour novels. An artificial, idealised world began to form inside her. Reality became for her a hateful thing, especially the reality of her household, where some ailing person was permanently clinging to her skirts. There followed her first acts of rebellion. She became harsh and impatient. She could not bear to be torn from the sentimental scenes in the book she was reading in order to help turn her husband over in bed and be obliged to smell his sour breath. The sight of medicine bottles, poultices and sores began to disgust her. She started reading poetry. She spent hours alone and silent at the window, and behind her fair virgin's gaze lay the rebellious thoughts of a woman of passion. She believed in lovers who climbed onto balconies with nightingales singing in the background, and she wanted to be loved like that, to be possessed by a lover on a dark, mysterious, romantic night.

Her love slowly detached itself from the image of Adrião and replaced him with a vague being made up of all the things that enchanted her about the heroes in novels, a being who was half-prince, half-felon, and who was, above all else, strong. Because that was what she admired and wanted, what she longed for on hot nights when she couldn't sleep – two arms as strong as steel to hold her in a mortal embrace, two lips of fire that would suck out her soul with a single kiss. She had become an hysteric.

Sometimes, standing by her husband's bed and seeing his consumptive, crippled body, she was filled with a dull hatred, a desire to hasten his death.

In the midst of this morbid excitement, the excitement of an overwrought temperament, she would be assailed by sudden weaknesses; she became as easily startled as a bird, would scream if a door slammed, would almost swoon if there were highly perfumed flowers in the room. At night, unable to breathe, she would fling open a window, but the warm air, the soft breath from the overheated earth would fill her with intense desire, with voluptuous longings interrupted by bouts of weeping.

The saint was turning into Venus.

So deeply had this morbid romanticism penetrated and corrupted her that there came a time when one touch from a man would have been enough for her to fall into his arms – and that is precisely what happened, two years later, with the first man who flirted with her. It was the apothecary.

The affair scandalised the whole town. And now she entirely neglects the house, leaves her children dirty, bleary-eyed and in rags, with nothing to eat until late at night, her husband calling out from his bedroom, the cloths for the poultices piled high on chairs, everything in a state of rank abandonment – and all to chase after that loathsome, greasy rascal, with his fat, bloated face, the thick ribbon of his black pince-nez tucked behind one ear and his little silk beret set at a jaunty angle.

He arrives at their late-night assignations wearing felt slippers and smelling of sweat; and he asks her for money to maintain a certain enormously fat creature called Joana, who is known in the town as the "Ball of Lard".

The Treasure

I

The three Medranhos brothers, Rui, Guanes and Rostabal, were the hungriest and most ragged noblemen in the whole kingdom of Asturias.

In their manor house, stripped of its windows and tiles by the mountain winds, they spent the winter evenings shivering in their goatskin jerkins, stamping the split soles of their boots on the cold flagstones in the kitchen, as they stood before the vast black fireplace where no fire had burned or saucepan bubbled for a very long time. When it grew dark, they would devour a crust of black bread rubbed with garlic, then, with no candle to light their way, trudge through the snow across the courtyard to go and sleep in the stable to take advantage of the warmth from their three scrawny mares, who, as starved as they were, were reduced to gnawing the wooden bars of the manger. Poverty had made these gentlemen as fierce as wolves.

One silent Sunday morning in Spring, when the three of them were scouring the Roquelanes woods for animal tracks and picking the occasional mushroom from among the oak trees, while their three mares grazed on the fresh April grass, the brothers came upon an old metal chest in a cave concealed behind a thicket of iron-wood trees. Its three keys were still in its three locks, as if it had been stored away in the safest of towers. On the lid, and barely decipherable beneath the rust, were two lines of verse in Arabic script. Inside, the chest was filled to the brim with gold doubloons!

In the terror and splendor of their excitement, the three noblemen turned as pale as wax. Then, plunging their hands wildly into the gold, they burst out laughing, and they laughed so loudly and so long that the tender leaves of the elms trembled. Then they drew back and, eyes ablaze, fixed each other with a look of such blatant distrust that Guanes and Rostabal both reached for the knives at their waist. Plump, fairhaired Rui, the most sensible of the brothers, raised his arms in arbitration and declared that this treasure, whether it came from God or the Devil, belonged to all three of them, and would be shared out equally once they had weighed the gold on a pair of scales. But how to carry that heavily-laden chest over the hills to Medranhos? And it would certainly not be wise to make off with their booty before nightfall. They therefore agreed that Guanes, who was the lightest of the three, should take some of the gold and hasten to the nearby village of Retortilho where he would buy three leather saddlebags, three sacks of barley, three meat pies and three bottles of wine. The pies and the wine were for them, because they hadn't eaten since the previous day; the barley was for the mares. And once restored, they would load the gold into the saddlebags, and men and beasts would return to Medranhos under cover of the moonless night.

'An excellent idea!' cried Rostabal, who was tall as a pine tree, had a great mane of hair, and a beard that grew from just beneath his bloodshot eyes to the buckle of his belt.

But Guanes wouldn't leave the chest; frowning and distrustful, he kept tugging with his fingers at the loose, swarthy skin of his crane-like neck. Then he announced gruffly:

'Brothers, the chest has three keys. I want to lock my lock

and take my key with me!

'Then I want mine too, damn it!' roared Rostabal.

Rui smiled. Of course, of course! Each of the three owners of the gold would have a key to keep. And so each brother crouched silently before the chest and turned his key in the lock. Reassured by this, Guanes leapt onto one of the mares and set off along the elm-lined path to Retortilho, serenading the trees with his usual mournful song:

¡Olé! ¡Olé!
Sale la cruz de la iglesia,
Vestida de negro luto…[1]

II

In the clearing where a thicket had once concealed the treasure chest (the three brothers having hacked the thicket down with their knives), a thread of water sprang up among the rocks and flowed onto a large concave stone, on which it formed a clear, still pool that slowly drained away into the tall grasses. Beside it, in the shade of a beech tree, lay what looked like an old fallen granite pillar covered in moss. There Rui and Rostabal sat down, keeping their hefty swords at the ready between their knees. The two mares were grazing on the lush grass, amid poppies and buttercups. In the branches above, a blackbird was singing. A smell of violets sweetened the bright air. Rostabal looked up at the sun and yawned with hunger.

Then Rui, who had taken off his hat and was smoothing

---

1 Olé, olé, the cross is leaving the church all draped in black mourning.

its battered red feathers, reminded Rostabal, in his soft, sensible tones, of how Guanes hadn't even wanted to come with them to the woods that morning, which really was most unfortunate! For if Guanes had stayed behind in Medranhos, only they would have discovered the chest and could then have shared the gold between them! It really was a terrible shame! Especially as Guanes would soon squander his share on women, gambling and drink.

'Ah, Rostabal, Rostabal, if Guanes had passed here on his own and found the gold, you can be sure that he would not have shared it with us!'

Rui gave an angry grunt and tugged at his black beard.

'No, damn it, you're right, Guanes *is* greedy! Do you remember how, last year, he won a hundred ducats from that swordsman from Fresno and wouldn't even lend me three ducats to buy a new jerkin!'

'You see!' cried Rui triumphantly.

Both had sprung up from the granite pillar, as if propelled by the same dazzling idea. And the tall grass whistled about their legs as they paced up and down.

'Besides, what is the point of him having all that gold?' Rui went on. 'Have you heard him coughing at night? The straw where he sleeps is black with the blood he coughs up. He won't last another winter, Rostabal! But by then he'll have frittered away all those good doubloons that should, by rights, be ours, so that we can repair our house, so that you can buy new horses, weapons, fine clothes, and pay your tithe as lord of the manor, as is only right and proper, you being the oldest of the Medranhos.'

'Let him die, then, let him die today!' roared Rostabal.

'Do you mean it?'

Rui had grabbed his brother's arm and was pointing to the

tree-lined path down which Guanes had departed, singing.

'There's the perfect place just over there, at the end of the path among the brambles. You must be the one to do it, Rostabal, because you're the strongest and the most skilled. A single blow with your sword and that will be that. And it's only fair that it should be you, because in the taverns, I've often heard Guanes refer to you openly as a pig and a dunce because you can't read or add up.'

'The wretch!'

'Let's go.'

Off they went and, when they reached the spot, they hid behind a large bramble bush growing beside the path, which was as narrow and stony as the bed of a stream. Down in the ditch, Rostabal had already unsheathed his sword. A light breeze shook the leaves of the poplars along the bank, and they could hear the faint ringing of the bells in Retortilho. Rui scratched his beard and calculated the hour by the sun, which was already beginning to sink towards the mountains. A flock of rooks passed overhead, cawing. And Rostabal, following their flight, began to yawn again with hunger, thinking about the pies and the wine that his brother would bring in his saddlebags.

At last, they heard, coming along the trail, the same hoarse, mournful song:

¡Olé!¡Olé!
Sale la cruz de la iglesia,
Toda vestida de negro...

Rui muttered: 'As soon as he passes, stab him in the side!'

The mare's hooves came clickclacking over the pebbles; the feather on his brother's hat bobbed, scarlet, above the brambles.

Rostabal burst out from behind the bush, wielding the long blade of his sword, which slipped easily into Guanes' side when, on hearing a noise, he turned in his saddle. He fell dully onto the stones. Rui had already grabbed the horse's reins, while Rostabal leapt upon Guanes, who was still gasping for breath, and repeatedly plunged his sword, which he held now as if it were a dagger, into his brother's chest and throat.

'Get his key!' yelled Rui.

And having wrenched the key from the dead man's breast, they both fled along the path, with Rostabal taking the lead, the feather on his hat all broken and bent, the bare blade of his sword tucked under his arm, and he still shuddering with disgust from the taste of the blood that had spurted into his mouth. Behind him, Rui was pulling desperately on the reins of the mare, which was digging its hooves into the stony ground and baring its long yellow teeth, unwilling to leave its master lying abandoned in the undergrowth.

To make her budge, he had to prod her thin flanks with the point of his sword and ended up, sword held high as if he were in pursuit of the Moor, galloping full pelt into the clearing, where the sun was no longer gilding the leaves. Rostabal had flung down hat and sword on the grass and was lying by the rock pool, sleeves rolled up, noisily washing his face and beard.

The mare, still laden with the new saddlebags Guanes had bought in Retortilho, was quiet now and had resumed her grazing. The necks of two bottles of wine protruded from the largest of the bags. Then Rui slowly drew his knife from his belt and, making not a sound on the thick grass, crept over to where Rostabal was still crouched by the pool, panting, his long beard dripping. And very calmly, as if he were driving a stake into a flower bed, Rui plunged the long blade into his brother's broad bent back, piercing his heart.

Rostabal fell face forwards into the pool without so much as a murmur, his long hair floating in the water. In order to get the third key, Rui had to turn the body over, and a rush of thick, steaming blood poured out and over the edge of the pool.

III

The three keys were all his! Rui stretched out his arms and took a deep, delicious breath. As soon as night fell, he would put the gold in the saddlebags and lead his three mares along the mountain paths up to Medranhos, where he would bury his treasure in the cellar. And when, beneath the December snows, only a few anonymous bones remained near the spring and further off among the brambles, he would be the magnificent lord of Medranhos and would have lavish masses said for his two dead brothers in the new chapel of the newly refurbished manor house. And if asked how they died. Why, as any Medranhos man should die – fighting the Turk!

He turned the keys in all three locks, grabbed a handful of doubloons, which he allowed to fall, jingling, onto the pebbles. Such pure gold, of the very finest quality! And it was *his* gold! He then went to see if the saddlebags would be large enough and, finding in one of them the two bottles of wine and a plump roasted capon, was suddenly filled with intense hunger. All he had eaten since yesterday was a sliver of dried fish. And it was a long time since he had tasted capon!

Delighted, he sat down on the grass and placed the delicious golden bird and the amber wine between his splayed legs.

Guanes had proved himself to be an excellent butler; he had even bought olives. But why only two bottles of wine, when there were three guests? He tore off a capon wing and sank his teeth into it. The sweet, pensive evening was coming on, with just a few pink clouds in the sky. Along the path, rooks were cawing. The mares, having eaten their fill of grass, were dozing, heads lowered. And the spring sang as it washed the dead man clean.

Rui raised the bottle to the light. Wine of such warmth and colour must have cost at least three *maravedis*. He put the neck of the bottle to his lips and drank in slow gulps that made the Adam's apple in his bearded throat rise and fall. Oh, blessed wine that so quickly warms the blood! He threw down the empty bottle and uncorked the second. However, being a sensible man, he did not drink from it; he needed to keep a clear head for the journey through the hills with his treasure. Resting on the grass, leaning on one elbow, he imagined the Medranhos mansion with its newly tiled roof, imagined himself on snowy evenings, sitting watching the tall flames of a blazing fire, imagined the brocaded bed where he would never lack for women.

Then, seized by a sudden anxiety, he hurriedly set about filling the saddlebags. The shadows among the trees were growing thicker. He led one of the mares over to the chest, lifted the lid, and took out a handful of doubloons. Then he hesitated and dropped the coins, which fell, tinkling, to the ground, while he pressed both hands to his breast. What is it, Don Rui? Great God! A fire, a bright fire had been lit inside him and was rising up into his throat! He tore open his jerkin, then swayed, panting, his tongue hanging out, as he wiped away great beads of sweat as cold as ice. Holy Mother of God! Then the wave of fire came again, stronger this time, sweeping through him, gnawing at his innards. He cried out:

'Help! Someone help! Guanes! Rostabal!'

In desperation, he beat the air with his contorted limbs. And inside him, the flames galloped ever higher; he could feel his bones cracking like the beams in a house on fire.

He staggered over to the spring to try and quench the flames, stumbling over Rostabal's body as he did so, scratching at the rock and howling with pain, and with one knee on the dead man's body, he scrabbled for a little of the water and splashed it on eyes and hair. But the water only burned him all the more, as if it were molten metal. He fell back onto the grass and, desperate for something cool to eat, grabbed whole fistfuls and crammed it in his mouth, biting his own fingers as he did so. He managed to get to his feet again, thick drool dribbling down his beard, and suddenly, eyes bulging horribly, he cried out, as if he had finally understood the full horror of the treachery:

'Poison!'

Yes, Don Rui, sensible Don Rui, it was poison! Because as soon as Guanes had arrived in Retortilho, even before he went to buy the saddlebags, he had run, singing, to an alleyway behind the cathedral in order to purchase from the old Jewish apothecary there the poison which, when mixed with wine, would make him the sole owner of the treasure.

Night fell. Two rooks from the cawing flock beyond the brambles further off had already alighted on Guanes' corpse. Meanwhile, the spring, still singing, continued to wash the other dead man clean. And half-buried in the dark grass, Rui's entire face had turned black. A single tiny star glimmered in the sky.

And the treasure is still there in the woods at Roquelanes.

Brother Juniper

I

At the time, the divine Francis of Assisi was still living alone in the Umbrian hills, and people throughout the whole of Italy were praising the saintliness of his friend and disciple, Brother Juniper.

Brother Juniper had, it is true, reached perfection in all the evangelical virtues. Through constant, copious prayer, he tore from his soul the tiniest roots of sin and left it as clean and innocent as one of those celestial gardens in which the soil is watered by the Lord and where only Madonna lilies grow. His penance, during the twenty years he had spent in the cloister, had been so harsh that he no longer feared the Tempter; and now he simply had to shake the sleeve of his habit to drive away temptations, however frightening or delicious, as if they were importunate flies. His charity, as beneficent and universal as the summer dew, did not fall only on the wretched poor, but on the melancholy rich as well. In his great humility, he considered himself not even the equal of a worm. The fierce barons, whose black towers dominated Italy, would bow their heads and reverently receive this patched and barefoot Franciscan, and he would preach gentleness to them. In Rome, in the Basilica of St John Lateran, Pope Honorius had kissed the wounds left by the chains that Brother Juniper had worn on his wrists during the year in which, out of love for the enslaved, he had himself endured slavery in the lands of the Moor. In those days, the angels still visited the Earth – concealing their wings, of course – and, staff in hand, they would follow the old pagan paths or stride through forests, and once, Brother Juniper actually met a young man of angelic, ineffable beauty, who smiled at him and murmured:

'Good morning, Brother Juniper!'

Now one day, while this admirable mendicant friar was travelling from Spoleto to Terni, he saw, silhouetted against the blue morning sky, on a hill thick with oak trees, the ruins of the castle of Otofrid, and his thoughts turned to his friend Egidio, a former novice, like himself, in the Monastery of Santa Maria degli Angeli, and who had withdrawn to that desolate place in order to be closer to God; and there he lived in a thatched hut beside the crumbling castle walls, singing as he watered the lettuces in his garden, for his was a sweet and gentle nature. More than three years had passed since Brother Juniper had last visited Egidio, and so he left the road and walked down into the valley, used the stepping stones to cross the stream that ran between the flowering oleander bushes, and then began the slow climb up the leafy hill. After the dust and heat of the road from Spoleto, the broad shade of the chestnut trees was a delight, as was the cool grass beneath his sore feet. Halfway up the hill, over a rock bristling with brambles, a thread of water whispered and glittered. Beside it, on the damp grass, snoring contentedly, lay a man, doubtless a swineherd, for he was wearing a heavy leather jerkin and had a swineherd's horn at his waist. The good brother drank a little water, flicked away the flies buzzing about the man's rough, sleeping face and continued on with his bag and his crook, giving thanks to God for the unexpected bounty of that water and that cool shade. Shortly afterwards, he came upon a herd of pigs snorting and snuffling about among the roots of the trees; some were thin and covered in coarse bristles, others were plump with short fat snouts, while the glossy, pink piglets scampered about, but never straying far from their mothers' teats.

Brother Juniper paused for a moment to consider the swineherd's lack of care and the real and dangerous possibility of wolves. Beyond the trees, however, lay the rocks and the ivy-choked remains of the Lombardy castle, where the sky was still visible through the occasional surviving embrasure and where, at one corner of a tower, a gutter in the form of a dragon's neck peered through the brambles.

The hermit's hut, thatched with straw anchored by stones, could just be seen among the dark granite rocks beyond the thriving vegetable garden with its cabbage beds and beanpoles and sweet-smelling lavender. Egidio could not be far away because he had left his water jug, pruning knife and hoe on the dry-stone wall. And so as not to disturb him, Brother Juniper very gently pushed open the door made of old planks, which Brother Egidio always kept hospitably unlocked.

'Brother Egidio!' he called.

A low moan came from the back of the rough cabin, which was more like the den of a wild beast.

'Who calls me? I'm here in this corner, dying, my brother, dying!'

Brother Juniper hurried anxiously over to him and found the good hermit lying on a pile of dry leaves; he was wrapped only in a few rags, and his face had grown so gaunt that his once plump, rosy cheeks, lost among the tufts of his white beard, were like very old, wrinkled parchment. With infinite charity and gentleness, Brother Juniper embraced him.

'But how long have you been in this terrible state, Brother Egidio?'

Praise God, Egidio said, only since the previous day, when, in the late afternoon, having taken one last look at the sun and at his garden, he had come and lain down in that corner to die. But for months now he had felt so tired that he could not even manage to carry a full pitcher of water back from the spring.

'But tell me, Brother Egidio, now that the Lord has brought me here, what can I do for your body? I ask only after your body, for your virtuous life spent in this wilderness has done more than enough for your soul.'

Moaning and clutching to his chest the dry leaves on which he was lying, as if they were the folds of a sheet, the poor hermit murmured:

'My good Brother Juniper, I'm not sure if it's a sin, but I must confess that all night I have thought of nothing but eating a slice of meat, a piece of roast pork. Is that a sin?'

In his mercy, Brother Juniper immediately reassured him. A sin? Certainly not! Anyone who denies his body an honest contentment merely to punish himself is acting in a manner displeasing to God. Did not Jesus tell his disciples to eat of the good things of the Earth? The body is a servant, and it is the Divine Will that it be fed and sustained so that it can do good and loyal service to the spirit, its master. When Brother Silvestre was very ill and felt a great desire for some moscatel grapes, good Francis of Assisi had immediately taken him to the vineyard and himself plucked the best bunches, having first blessed them to make them still sweeter and juicier.

'So it's a piece of roast pork you fancy!' exclaimed Brother Juniper cheerily, stroking the hermit's almost transparent hands. 'Fear not, dear brother, I know how to grant your wish.'

His eyes shining with charity and love, he immediately took the sharp pruning knife from the garden wall and, rolling up the sleeves of his habit, and as lightly as a deer, because what he was about to do was in the service of the Lord, he ran down the hill to the thick chestnut trees where he had found the herd of pigs. And after walking stealthily from trunk to trunk, he came upon a lone piglet grubbing for acorns. He pounced on it, closing one hand around its snout to muffle its squeals, while, with the other, he neatly chopped off one of its legs with two deft strokes of the pruning knife. Then, with his hands bespattered with gore, with the piglet's leg still dripping, the kindly man left the creature breathing its last in a pool of its own blood, raced up the hill to the cabin and shouted gaily to Brother Egidio inside:

'Brother Egidio, the good Lord has given us the piece of meat you wanted! And during my time at Santa Maria degli Angeli, I became quite a good cook.'

He took a stake from the hermit's garden and sharpened one end with the still bloody pruning knife. Between two stones he lit a fire and over it eagerly, lovingly roasted the leg of pork. So charitable was he that, in order to give Egidio the full flavour of that banquet, so rare in that world of mortification, he called to him cheerfully, temptingly:

'The meat is browning nicely, Brother Egidio! The skin is crisping well, dear saint!'

Then he made a triumphant entry into the hut, bearing the steaming and delicious roast pork, served on a bed of lettuce leaves. He tenderly helped the old man to sit up, for Brother Egidio was trembling and dribbling with greed. He pushed back from his friend's poor, emaciated face the locks of hair that had become stuck to his skin with sweat. And so that Brother Egidio would not feel embarrassed by his own voracious and very carnal appetite, he told him, as he cut up the meat for him, that he would have happily shared some of that excellent pork if he hadn't already dined lavishly at the local inn.

'I couldn't eat another mouthful now, Brother! I stuffed myself with a whole chicken, followed by some fried eggs! Not to mention a carafe of white wine!'

The saintly man was telling a saintly lie, for since dawn, he had enjoyed only a bowl of thin broth given to him as alms at the gate of a farm.

Sated and satisfied, Egidio sighed and fell back on his bed of dry leaves. It had done him so much good! The Lord, in his justice, would reward Brother Juniper for that piece of pork! He even felt that his soul was better prepared now for the fearful journey. The hermit then put his hands together in prayer, and Brother Juniper knelt down beside him, and both gave fervent thanks to God, who sends succour from afar to meet the needs of the solitary.

Then, having covered Egidio with a scrap of blanket and placed beside him a pitcher of cool water, and hung a piece of cloth at the window as a protection against the cool evening breezes, Brother Juniper bent over him and said softly:

'My dear brother, you cannot stay here all alone. I must leave now on Jesus's business, which cannot wait, but I will stop at the convent of Sambricena and leave a message for a novice to come and tend to you in your final days. May God watch over you until then, my brother. May God console and protect you with His right hand!'

But Egidio had closed his eyes, and did not even move; perhaps he had fallen asleep or, having paid his body its final wage, as one would a good servant, perhaps his spirit had departed for ever, his work on Earth completed. Brother Juniper blessed the old man, took up his staff and walked back down the hill through the oak woods. The swineherd's horn was now furiously blaring forth the alarm, for the man had doubtless woken up and found the mutilated piglet. Brother Juniper quickened his pace, thinking how magnanimous the Lord was in allowing a man, made in His august image, to be so easily consoled by a leg of pork roasted over a fire lit between two stones.

He returned to the road and continued on to Terni. And from that day forth, his virtuous works were many and prodigious. He preached the Eternal Gospel throughout the whole of Italy, making the rich more charitable and enlarging the hopes of the poor. His immense love reached beyond those who suffer to those who sin, offering a salve for every sorrow, forgiving every guilty secret; and he converted bandits with the same degree of charity with which he healed lepers. During the harsh snows of winter, he often gave his tunic and sandals to beggars, for there were always abbots of wealthy monasteries or devout ladies who would clothe him again, so as to avoid the scandal of him walking naked through their cities; and then, if he came across some other poor wretch in rags, he would smilingly give him those new garments. To liberate serfs from cruel masters and buy their freedom, he would go into churches and take the silver candelabra from the altar, declaring cheerfully that God is better pleased by a free soul than by a burning torch.

Surrounded by widows and starving children, he would invade bakeries, butcher's shops and even pawnshops, where he would imperiously demand, in the name of God, that the disinherited be given their just deserts. For him, suffering and humiliation were sources of great joy: nothing delighted him more than arriving at night, starving, shivering and soaked to the skin, at the door of some opulent feudal abbey and being driven away like a vagabond; only then, crouched in the mud by the roadside, chewing on a handful of herbs, did he feel that he was truly a brother of Jesus, who, like him and unlike the beasts of the field, had neither a hole nor a nest in which to take shelter. One day, in Perugia, his fellow friars came to meet him, bearing festive banners and with the bells ringing; his response was to run over to a dungheap and roll about in it, soiling his clothes, so that those who came to raise him up would feel only compassion and scorn. Whether in the cloister, the open countryside, in the midst of multitudes, or during the fiercest of battles, he would pray constantly, not out of duty, but because he took such delight in prayer. He took even greater delight, however, in teaching and serving others. And thus he spent long years wandering among men, pouring forth his heart like the waters of a river, offering his own arms as tireless levers; and he was as glad to help an old lady on some barren hillside carry her load of firewood as he was to walk, unarmed, into a city in revolt, full of clashing swords and spears, in the hope that he might bring peace where there was discord.

Then one afternoon, just before Easter, he was resting on the steps of Santa Maria degli Angeli, when he suddenly saw a vast shining hand reaching down through the smooth, pale air. He murmured thoughtfully:

'That is the hand of God, His right hand, reaching out either to welcome or reject me.'

He immediately gave his last remaining possession – a very worn, tear-stained copy of the Gospel – to the poor man sitting nearby who was saying a Hail Mary, his pouch for alms on his lap. On the following Sunday, in church, at the raising of the Host, Brother Juniper fainted. Sensing then that he was nearing the end of his earthly journey, he asked to be taken to a stable or to be laid on a bed of ashes.

However, in holy obedience to the guardian of the convent,

he agreed that the rags he was wearing should be removed and replaced with a new habit; his eyes filled with tears, though, and he begged, at least, to be buried in a borrowed tomb, just like Jesus, his Lord.

His one complaint, he said with a sigh, was that he felt no pain.

'O Lord, who suffered so, why do you not send me the same blessed suffering?'

At dawn, he asked them to open wide the doors of the stable.

He contemplated the brightening sky, listened to the swallows, who, in the coolness and silence, were beginning to twitter under the eaves, and recalled with a smile a similarly cool, silent morning when, walking with Francis of Assisi beside Lake Trasimeno, that incomparable teacher had stopped beneath a tree full of roosting birds and fraternally urged them to praise the Lord unceasingly! 'My brother birds, sing sweetly to your Creator, who gave you this tree that you might live in it and this clean water that you might drink, and those warm feathers to protect you and your children!' Then, humbly kissing the sleeve of the monk tending him, Brother Juniper died.

II

As soon as he closed his fleshly eyes, a great diaphanous angel entered the stable and took the soul of Brother Juniper in his arms. In the fine dawn light, the angel slipped so lightly across the meadow opposite that he did not even touch the dewy tips of the tall grass. Then, opening radiant, snow-white wings, he calmly flew through the clouds and beyond the stars and sky known to mankind.

Nestled in the angel's arms, as if gently rocked in a cradle, Brother Juniper's soul had retained the form of the body it had left behind on Earth; it was still clothed in the Franciscan habit, with a little dust and ash clinging to its rough folds; and with new eyes, which could now penetrate and understand everything, his astonished soul contemplated the place where the angel had stopped, far beyond transitory universes and mere sidereal murmurings. It was a space without limits, shape or colour. Up above, a glow, like a sunrise, was growing brighter and more radiant until it shone with a light so sublime that, beside it, the most brilliant sun would seem but a brownish smudge. And beneath lay a darkness that grew ever duller, gloomier, greyer, until it formed a thick, crepuscular, fathomless sadness. The angel hovered, waiting, his wings folded, between that upper brightness and that lower darkness. And Brother Juniper's soul knew that it, too, was hovering between Purgatory and Paradise. Then, suddenly, from the heights, there appeared the two vast pans of a pair of scales – one shone like a diamond and was reserved for his Good Works, while the other, blacker than coal, was there to receive the weight of his Bad Deeds. In the angel's enfolding arms, Juniper's soul shuddered. Then the diamond-bright pan began slowly to descend! What contentment, what glory! Laden with his Good Works, it descended calmly and majestically, radiating light. So heavy was it that its thick cords creaked under the weight. And in the pan itself, forming a kind of mountain of snow, his evangelical virtues glowed white. There were the countless small gifts of money he had scattered throughout the world and which had blossomed into white flowers full of perfume and light.

His humility was a mountain peak haloed by intense light. Every one of his penances glittered more brightly than the purest crystals. And his perennial prayers rose and coiled about the cords, like a dazzling golden mist.

Serene and majestic as a star, the pan holding its precious cargo of Good Works finally halted. High above, the other pan still did not move, but hung there, coal-black, empty, useless and forgotten. Sonorous bands of seraphim were already flying up from the depths, waving green palm leaves. The humble Franciscan friar was about to make his triumphal entry into Paradise, and they were the divine militia who would accompany him, singing. A tremor of joy ran through the light of Paradise, which was about to be enriched by a new saint. And Brother Juniper's soul experienced a foretaste of Bliss.

Suddenly, however, the black pan trembled as if an unexpected weight had fallen into it! And then, implacably, it began to descend, casting a grim shadow over the celestial brilliance all around. What Bad Deed did it bear, so small that it couldn't be seen, but so heavy that it was forcing the other, luminous pan to rise up, as if the mountain of Good Works with which it was overflowing were nothing but mendacious smoke? Oh, the pain, the despair! The seraphim drew back, their wings trembling. A great wave of terror swept through Brother Juniper's soul. Steadily and inexorably, the black pan was descending, its cords taut. And in the grey, inconsolably sad place that swirled beneath the angel's feet, a mass of darkness softly, soundlessly rose and fell, approached and withdrew, like the waves of a devouring tide.

The pan, sadder than the night itself, had stopped in horrible equilibrium with its shining other half. And the seraphim, Juniper, and the angel who had brought him there discovered, lying at the bottom of that pan, a little pig, a poor piglet panting and dying in a pool of its own blood, one leg barbarously cut off. That mutilated creature weighed as heavily in the scales of justice as a whole bright mountain of perfect virtues!

From on high came a vast hand, its spread fingers glittering. It was the hand of God, His right hand, the same that had appeared to Brother Juniper on the steps of Santa Maria degli Angeli and which was once again reaching down either to welcome or reject him. Both the light and the dark, from dazzling Paradise to darkling Purgatory, shrank back in a movement of inexpressible love and terror. And in that moment of ecstatic silence, the vast hand reaching down from on high made a gesture of rejection.

Bowing his pitying head, the angel opened his arms and let the soul of Brother Juniper fall into the darkness of Purgatory.

The Wet Nurse

Once upon a time there was a valiant young king who ruled over a kingdom abundant in cities and lands, but who had ridden off to do battle in some far-off country, leaving his queen and his little son – still in his cradle, still in his swaddling clothes – alone and sad.

The full moon that had seen him leave, borne away by his dream of conquest and fame, was already beginning to wane when one of his knights returned, black with dried blood and with dust from the road, his sword and spear broken; he brought the bitter news of a battle lost and of a king, his body pierced by seven spears, lying slain beside a great river, together with the very flower of his noblemen.

The queen mourned the king magnificently. She wept even more desolately for her handsome, cheerful husband. Above all, though, she cried desperately for the father who had thus left his little son all unguarded, with no strong, loving arm to protect him, and surrounded by the many enemies of his fragile life and of the kingdom that would one day be his.

Of those enemies, the boldest was his uncle, the king's bastard brother, a cruel, depraved man, consumed by gross envy, whose sole reason for wanting the throne was to gain possession of its treasures, and who had, for years, lived in a castle in the mountains with his horde of rebels, like a wolf watching from above for its prey. The prey, alas, was that little child, that nurseling king, the lord of many provinces, who lay asleep in his cradle, clutching his golden rattle!

Beside him, slept another child in another cradle. He, however, was only a slave, the baby son of the lovely, robust slave girl who was wet nurse to the prince. They had both been born on the same summer night and the same breast had fed them. When the queen, before going to bed, came to kiss the little prince, who had fine, fair hair, she also fondly kissed the little slave, whose hair was dark and curly. Both children had eyes that shone like gemstones, but while the prince's cradle was a magnificent thing of ivory and brocade, the slave-boy's simple cradle was made of wicker. The loyal wet nurse, however, showered both with equal affection, because while one was her son, the other would be her king.

She had been born in the royal household, and her passion and her religion were her king and queen. No more heartfelt tears than hers had flowed for that king slain on the banks of the great river. She belonged, however, to a race that believed in the continuance of our earthly life in Heaven. The king, her master, would no doubt now be ruling over another kingdom beyond the clouds, one equally abundant in cities and lands. His horse, his weapons and his pages would have risen up with him into the heights, and his vassals, when they died, would promptly ascend to that celestial kingdom where they would resume their vassalage. And one day, she, in turn, would be carried up on a ray of light to inhabit her master's palace and once again spin the linen for his tunics and light the incense burner in his room, and she would be as happy in her servitude in Heaven as she had been on Earth.

And yet she, too, trembled for her little prince! How often, when she held him at her breast, did she ponder his fragility, his long childhood, the slow years that must pass before he was even the height of a sword, and she would think of that cruel, power-hungry uncle, whose face was darker than the night and whose heart was darker than his face, and who was always watching from atop his mountain, surrounded by the scimitars wielded by his horde! Her poor beloved prince! She clasped him still more tenderly to her, but her own son babbled away beside him, and it was to him that her arms reached out most eagerly and happily. He, being poor, had nothing to fear from life. Misfortunes and ill luck could never leave him more bereft of the glories and wealth of the world than he was now, there in his cradle, with only a scrap of white linen to cover his nakedness. Indeed, his life was more precious and far worthier of being preserved than that of the prince, because none of the harsh cares that cast a shadow on the soul of the powerful would touch his free and simple slave's soul. And as if she loved him all the more for his blessedly humble state, she would cover his plump body with long, devouring kisses, unlike the brief kisses she bestowed on the hands of her prince.

Meanwhile, a great mood of dread filled the palace, where a woman now ruled among women. The bastard brother, that predatory man who roamed the mountains, had come down to the plain with his hordes and was already leaving a trail of death and destruction in the once happy villages and hamlets. The gates of the city were secured with stronger chains. Bonfires burned on the watchtowers. But their defences lacked manly discipline. A rock cannot govern like a sword. All the nobles faithful to the throne had perished in the great battle. And the unfortunate queen could do nothing but run again and again to the cradle of her little son and bemoan her widow's weakness. Only the loyal wet nurse seemed confident, as if the arms with which she clasped the prince to her were the walls of a citadel that no bold enemy could penetrate.

Now, one dark and silent night, when she was already undressed and about to get into the truckle bed that stood between the cradles of her two little boys, she sensed rather than heard the faint, distant clamour of clashing steel in the royal gardens. Quickly wrapping a blanket about her and drawing back her hair, she listened anxiously. Rough, heavy feet were running across the sandy ground among the jasmine bushes. Then came a groan and the sound of a body falling dully onto the flagstones, like a bundle of clothes. She violently drew aside the curtain. And there, at the far end of the gallery, she saw men, the flash of lanterns and the glint of weapons. In that second, she understood everything: the palace walls had been breached, and the cruel bastard brother had come to steal and kill her prince! Without a moment's hesitation or doubt, she snatched the prince from his ivory cot and placed him in the poorer one, and taking her son from his slave's cradle, all the while bestowing on him desperate kisses, she laid him in the royal cradle, which she covered with brocade.

Suddenly, at the door of the room, there appeared a huge man with a scarlet face, and wearing a black cloak over his coat of mail. He was accompanied by other men bearing lanterns. He peered in, then ran to the ivory and brocaded cradle, plucked up the child as if he were stealing a purse of gold and, muffling the child's cries with his cloak, ran furiously away.

The prince slept on in his new cradle, and the wet nurse was left alone in the silence and the dark.

However, cries of alarm now echoed through the palace. Outside, she could see the tall flames of torches. The courtyards rang with the clank of steel. And almost naked, her hair wild, the queen rushed into the room, along with her maids, calling out for her son. When she saw the ivory cradle empty and the bedclothes all awry, she dropped to the floor, weeping and distraught. Then, without a word, the wet nurse, looking deathly pale, very slowly uncovered the other cradle. There was the prince, sleeping soundly, dreaming a dream that lit up his face and his golden curls and made him smile. With a sigh, the queen fell face forwards onto the cradle, as if dead.

And at that moment, a renewed clamour shook the marble gallery. It was the captain of the guard, the queen's faithful men. However, there was in his voice more sadness than triumph. The bastard brother was dead. Caught, as he escaped, between the palace and the citadel, and surrounded by their many archers, he and twenty of his men had finally succumbed. His body, pierced by arrows, was still lying there in a pool of blood. But, alas, O unspeakable grief! The tender little body of the prince lay there too, wrapped in a cloak, quite cold, his face still purple from the fierce hands that had strangled him! As her men-at-arms were, as one, giving her this cruel news, the queen, eyes ablaze, half-weeping, half-smiling, held up, for all to see, her prince, who had now awoken.

There was general amazement and acclamation. Who had saved him? Who? There, stiff and silent beside the empty ivory cradle, stood his saviour, that sublimely loyal servant, who, in order to preserve the prince's life had sent her own son to his death. Then, and only then, did the happy queen emerge from her ecstatic joy and passionately embrace the grieving mother and kiss her, calling her 'dearest sister'. And from among the multitude crammed into the gallery there came a new, more ardent cry, calling for a lavish reward to be given to the admirable servant who had saved both king and kingdom.

But how? What bags of gold could possibly repay her for her son's life? Then an old nobleman suggested that she be taken to see the royal treasure so that she could choose whatever she wanted from among those marvels, the finest that India could offer. The queen took her servant by the hand. And the wet nurse, her marble face still rigid with grief, and walking as if she were dead or in a dream, was led to the treasure chamber. Ladies and gentlemen, maids and men-at-arms followed in such profound, respectful silence that one could not even hear the slap of sandal on flagstone. The heavy doors of the treasure chamber rolled slowly open. And when a servant unbarred the windows, the bright, rosy, dawn light that came flooding in between the iron bars ignited a marvellous, glittering fire of gold and precious stones! From the stone floor to the dark vault of the ceiling, the entire room was filled with a brilliant, coruscating, sparkling array of gold sovereigns, ornate inlaid weapons, heaps of diamonds, piles of coins, long strings of pearls, all the wealth of the kingdom accumulated by a hundred kings over twenty centuries. A long, slow 'Ah!' ran through the otherwise dumbstruck crowd. There followed an anxious silence. And in the middle of the chamber, surrounded by all that refulgent splendour, the wet nurse did not move except to raise her tearless, shining eyes to that pink- and gold-tinged sky beyond the bars. Her little boy was up there in that cool morning sky. Yes, there he was, and the sun was rising and it was getting late, and her child would doubtless be crying and wanting her breast! Then she smiled and reached out her hand. Everyone held their breath as they followed the slow movement of her open hand. What marvellous jewel, what string of diamonds, what fistful of rubies would she choose?

She reached out her hand, and from a stool piled high with splendid weapons, she chose an emerald-encrusted dagger. It had once belonged to a king and was worth a whole province.

She picked up the dagger and gripping it firmly in her hand, pointed up to the heavens, where the first rays of sun were just appearing. Then, turning to face the queen and the crowd, she cried:

'I saved my prince and now I am going to suckle my son!'

And with that, she drove the dagger through her heart.

The Sweet Miracle

At the time, Jesus had still not left Galilee or the sweet, luminous shores of Lake Tiberias, but news of his miracles had reached as far as Engannim, a wealthy city with strong walls and set among olive groves and vineyards in the land of Issachar.

One afternoon, a man with wide, burning eyes arrived in that cool valley and announced that a new prophet, a marvellous teacher capable of curing all human ills was visiting the fields and villages of Galilee preaching the coming of the Kingdom of God. And while the man rested beside the Fountain of the Gardens, he told, too, how that same teacher, on the road to Magdala, had cured of leprosy the servant of a Roman decurion, simply by stretching his hand over him; and that on another day, while crossing by boat to the land of the Gerasenes, where the balsam harvest was just beginning, he had restored to life the daughter of Jairus, who was a learned and respected man and an elder in the synagogue. And when the astonished labourers and shepherds and the dusky women carrying their water pitchers asked if that man was, indeed, the Messiah of Judea, and if a sword of fire went before him, and if he was flanked by the shadows of Gog and Magog, like two towers, the man, without even drinking the cold water of which Joshua had once drunk, picked up his stick, shook out his hair and set off thoughtfully under the aqueduct and was soon lost among the almond trees thick with blossom. But a hope – as delicious as the dew in the months when the crickets sing –

refreshed those simple souls; across the fertile plain as far as Ashkelon, the plough seemed to cut more easily through the soil and the olive press was easier to work; children, picking anemones, peered down the roads to see if, beyond the wall or beneath the sycamore, some great light would appear; and on the stone benches at the gates of the city, the old men, stroking their beards, no longer trotted out the old maxims with quite the same wise certainty.

Now there lived in Engannim an old man called Obed, who belonged to a noble family from Samaria. He had sacrificed on the altars of Mount Ebal and was the owner of many flocks and many vineyards, and his heart was as full of pride as his granary was of wheat. However, a dry, scorching wind, like the desolating wind which, at the Lord's command, blows from the sinister lands of Essur, had killed the fattest sheep in his flocks, and on the slopes where his vines had once twined about the elm trees and up elegant trellises there were only shrivelled stumps and leaves gnawed by rust. Crouched at the door of his house, sieving the dust through his fingers and with one corner of his cloak pulled down over his face, Obed bemoaned his old age and mentally excoriated God for his cruelty.

When he heard about this new teacher from Galilee, who could feed whole multitudes, drive out demons, and heal all ills, Obed, who was a well-read man and had travelled in Phoenicia, immediately assumed that Jesus was one of those miracle-workers so common in Palestine, such as Apollonius or Rabbi Ben-Dossa or Simon the Subtle. Such men could converse with the stars even on dark, overcast nights and always found their secrets clear and easily decipherable; with one wave of a wand they could drive from the fields horseflies bred in the mud of Egypt and grasp with their fingers the edge of the shadows cast by trees and, in the noonday heat, draw them over the threshing floor like kindly awnings. Being a younger man, Jesus of Galilee was doubtless possessed of a still more potent magic, and would, if paid well, stop Obed's flocks from dying and would turn his vineyards green again. Obed ordered his servants to go forth and scour the whole of Galilee for this new teacher and lure him back to Engannim in the land of Issachar with the promise of money or jewellery.

The servants tightened their leather belts and set off down the road that the caravans followed along the lakeshore as far as Damascus. One evening, as the sun was setting, as red and ripe as a pomegranate, they saw the lovely snows of Mount Hermon. Later, one cool, soft morning, Lake Tiberias lay resplendent before them, transparent, silent, bluer than the sky itself, and edged with verdant meadows, fertile gardens, porphyry rocks and white roof-terraces set amid palm trees and flights of doves. A fisherman, who was idly untying his boat from a grassy mooring shaded by oleanders, listened with a smile to the servants' question. The teacher from Nazareth? He had left with his disciples in the month of Iyar to go to the lands into which the Jordan flows.

The servants hurried off, following the banks of the river as far as the ford where the river broadens out to form a pool and, for a moment, sleeps there, green and motionless, in the shade of the tamarinds. On the bank, an Essene, all dressed in white linen and holding a white lambkin in his arms, was delicately picking health-giving herbs. The servants greeted him humbly, for such men are much beloved of the people, because their hearts are as clean and clear and candid as their clothes, which they wash each morning in pure water. Did he know the whereabouts of the new teacher from Galilee, who, like the Essenes, preached gentleness and cured both people and animals? The Essene said softly that the teacher had crossed the oasis of Engaddi and then travelled onward. But where? With the sprig of purple flowers he had picked, the Essene pointed to the lands on the other side of the Jordan, to the plain of Moab. The servants forded the river and trudged along rough tracks, as far as the rocks below the grim citadel of Makaur, but in vain. At Jacob's Well, they came upon a long caravan carrying myrrh and spices and balsam from Gilead to Egypt. The camel-drivers, drawing up water in leather buckets, told Obed's servants that in Gadara, around the time of the new moon, a marvellous teacher, greater even than David or Isaiah, had cast out seven demons from the breast of a weaver-woman and that, at a word from him, a man whose throat had been slit by the thief Barrabas had risen from his tomb and returned to work in his vegetable garden. Filled with hope, Obed's servants immediately set off along the pilgrim route to Gadara, a city of high towers, and beyond that, to the springs of Al Malha. There, however, they learned that Jesus, followed by a crowd singing and waving branches of mimosa, had embarked that morning on a fishing boat to cross the lake to Magdala. Greatly discouraged, Obed's servants again crossed the Jordan at the Bridge of Jacob's Daughters, and eventually, their sandals battered and torn, reached Roman Judea, where they met a grave-faced Pharisee returning to Ephraim on his mule. With all due reverence, they stopped that man of the Law. Had he, by any chance, met this new prophet from Galilee, who sowed miracles about him like a god strolling the Earth? The face of the hook-nosed Pharisee darkened and scowled, and his angry response thundered about him like a proud drum:

'You pagan slaves! You blasphemers! Who told you that there are prophets or miracles outside of Jerusalem! Jehovah alone reigns in his Temple! Only fools and impostors come from Galilee!'

And when the servants recoiled before his raised fist, all twined about with sacred symbols, the furious scholar leapt from his mule and stoned them with the stones from the road, roaring: 'Racca! Racca!' and heaping upon them all the ritual anathemas. The servants fled back to Engannim. And great was Obed's despair, for his animals were still dying and his vineyards withering, while, as radiant as the dawn light behind the mountains, the fame of Jesus of Galilee continued to grow and to provide a source of consolation and divine promises.

Around that time, a Roman centurion, Publius Septimus, was in command of the fort guarding the vale of Caesarea, from the city down to the sea. Publius, a harsh man and a veteran of Tiberius' campaign against the Parthians, had, during the Samarian revolt, grown rich on prisoners and pillage and even owned mines in Attica, and, as if it were a supreme favour bestowed by the gods, he also enjoyed the friendship of Flaccus, the imperial legate of Syria. But a great grief gnawed at his power and prosperity, the way a worm gnaws at a succulent fruit. His only daughter, whom he loved more than life or wealth, was dying from a slow, subtle illness, unknown even to the physicians and magicians whose advice he sought in Sidon and Tyre. Pale and sad as a moon over a cemetery, she was slowly dying, yet she uttered not a word of complaint, but only smiled wanly at her father as she sat beneath an awning on the fort's high esplanade, her sad, dark eyes gazing longingly out at the blue sea of Tyre, across which she had sailed from Italy on a fine galley. At her side, a legionnaire standing on the ramparts would sometimes idly aim his arrow upwards and pierce a great eagle flying on serene wings across the dazzling sky. Septimus's daughter would, for a moment, follow the eagle's tumbling body until it landed dead on the rocks, then, sadder still and paler, she would sigh and again look out to sea.

When Septimus heard the merchants of Chorazim talking about this admirable teacher, who had such power over minds that he could heal the dark ills of the soul, he despatched three decuria of soldiers to search the whole of Galilee and the ten cities of the Decapolis as far as the coast and as far as Ashkelon. The soldiers put their shields away in canvas bags and stuck sprigs of olive on their helmets, and soon their iron-studded sandals were echoing over the basalt flagstones of the Roman road that traversed the whole tetrarchy of Herod, from Caesarea to the lake. At night, their weapons glinted on the top of hills, among the flickering flames of their torches. By day, they invaded villages, scoured dense orchards, pierced haystacks with their spears; and the frightened women sought to placate them with honey cakes, fresh figs and bowls of wine that the soldiers downed in one as they sat in the shade of the sycamores. Thus they searched the whole of Lower Galilee, and the only trace they found of the teacher was the luminous furrow left in men's hearts. Weary of these pointless marches and convinced that the Jews were hiding their miracle-worker so that the Romans would not benefit from his superior magic, they gave terrible vent to their anger throughout that pious, submissive land. They would stop pilgrims on bridges and shout out the teacher's name; they tore the veils from virgins' faces; and at the hour when people were filling their water jugs at the wells, they would rush through the narrow streets of towns, burst into synagogues and with the hilt of their swords strike the Tebah, the holy cedar ark containing the Sacred Books. Near Hebron, they dragged hermits from their caves by their beards in order to force from them the name of the desert or oasis where the teacher was hiding, and two Phoenician merchants travelling from Joppa with a load of spikenard, and who had never even heard the name of Jesus, were forced to pay each decurion one hundred drachma for that crime of ignorance. The country people, even the bold shepherds of Idumaea, who provide the Temple with sacrificial lambs, all fled in terror into the mountains as soon as, at some turn in the road, they spotted the glinting weapons of that violent band. And standing at the edge of threshing-floors, old women tore at their dishevelled hair and heaped ill luck upon the soldiers, invoking the vengeance of Elijah. Thus the soldiers continued their erratic, tumultuous wanderings as far as Ashkelon, but still they did not find Jesus, and so they withdrew to the coast, where their sandals sank into the burning sands.

One day, near Caesarea, just before dawn, they were marching along a valley and saw, on a hillside, a dark green laurel wood, where they spotted the modest white portico of a temple. Standing on the marble steps, gravely waiting for the sun to rise, was an old man with a long white beard, he was wearing a laurel wreath and a saffron-coloured robe and holding a small three-stringed lyre. Down below, waving an olive branch, the soldiers shouted up to the priest. Did he know of a new prophet from Galilee, who was so skilled at miracles that he could bring the dead back to life and change water into wine? The serene old gentleman spread wide his arms and called back over the dewy green valley:

'Do you Romans really believe that any miracle-working prophets could come out of Galilee or Judaea? How can a barbarian change the order instituted by Zeus? Magicians and miracle-workers are mere peddlars uttering hollow words in order to wheedle money out of simpletons. Without the permission of the immortals not even a dead branch may fall from a tree nor can a dry leaf be shaken from a bough. There are no prophets! There are no miracles! Only Delphic Apollo knows the secret of all things!'

Then slowly, heads bowed, as if after a defeat in battle, the soldiers withdrew to the fortress of Caesarea, and great was the despair of Publius Septimus because his daughter continued to die without complaint while gazing out at the sea of Tyre; meanwhile, the fame of Jesus, healer of such lingering ailments, continued to grow, and his was an ever more consoling fame, as refreshing as the evening breeze that blows down from Mount Hermon and through the gardens, where it restores to life the drooping lilies.

Now between Engannim and Caesarea, in a solitary shack, deep in the fold of a hill, there lived a widow, the most wretched of all the women in Israel. Her one son was crippled, and had passed from the scrawny breast at which she had suckled him to the ragged sheets of a filthy mattress, where for seven years he had lain, moaning and slowly withering away. Illness was gnawing at her as well in the rags she never changed, for she was darker and more twisted than an uprooted vine stock. And poverty grew on them both as thickly as lichen on potshards lost in the wilderness. Even the oil in the red clay lamp had long since dried up. In the painted chest there was neither a grain of wheat nor a crust of bread. In the summer, the goat had died for lack of grass to eat, and then the fig-tree in the garden had shrivelled and died too. Living far from any village, the woman never received at her door the alms of bread or honey. And so in that Chosen Land, where even birds of ill omen had more than enough to eat, those children of God survived on the weeds that grew among the rocks and which the woman cooked without so much as a pinch of salt.

One day, a beggar arrived at the shack and shared what food he had with the poor, sad mother, and while sitting by the fireside, scratching the wounds on his leg, he spoke of a great hope for all those who were lonely and forlorn, a teacher who had appeared in Galilee and who could make six loaves where there had been only one and who promised the poor a great kingdom of light, more splendid even than Solomon's court. The woman listened with hungry eyes. And where was he to be found that gentle teacher, the hope of the lonely and forlorn? The beggar sighed. Ah, how many had sought him and how many had despaired! His fame had spread throughout Judaea, like the sunlight that falls on even the oldest wall; but only those fortunate few whom he himself chose could see his bright face. Wealthy Obed had sent his servants throughout Galilee to find Jesus and lure him to Engannim with promises; powerful Publius Septimus had sent his soldiers as far as the coast to search for Jesus and order him to return with them to Caesarea. On his travels, begging for alms along the roads, the man had met both Obed's servants and Publius Septimus' legionnaires. And they had all gone home defeated, their sandals worn out, without ever discovering in which forest or city, in which cave or palace, Jesus was hiding.

Evening was coming on. The beggar took up his stick and walked back down the rough path through the heather and the rocks. That bent, abandoned mother returned to her corner. And then her son, in a voice as faint as the rustle of a bird's wing, asked his mother to bring him that teacher who loved children, however poor, and who healed all ills, however old. His mother clutched her dishevelled head and cried:

'My child, how can I leave you and set off in search of that teacher from Galilee? Obed is rich, and yet his servants searched in vain for Jesus by the seashore and among hills, from Chorazim to the land of Moab. Publius Septimus is powerful and has soldiers at his command, and in vain they pursued Jesus from Hebron to the sea. How can I possibly leave you? Jesus is far away and our griefs live with us here within these walls, imprisoning us. And even if I did find him, how could I convince a teacher so desired by so many, for whom even the rich and the powerful sigh, to travel from the cities to this desolate place to heal a little cripple lying on a poor, wretched mattress?'

Two tears ran down the child's thin face, and he murmured:

'But, Mama, Jesus loves all the little children. And I'm still only little and have this terrible disease, and I so want to get better!'

And his mother answered, sobbing:

'Oh, my child, how can I leave you? The roads to Galilee are long and men's pity is brief. I'm so broken, so frail, so wretched that even the dogs at the entrance to the villages would bark at me. No one would listen to my plea or tell me where the gentle teacher lives. My child, perhaps Jesus is dead. After all, not even the rich and the powerful could find him. Heaven brought him and Heaven took him away. And with him die the hopes of the lonely and forlorn for ever.'

From among the black rags that served him as blankets, the child held up his trembling hands and murmured:

'But, Mama, I want to see Jesus…'

And then, slowly opening the door and smiling, Jesus said to the child:

'Here I am.'

Recommended Reading

If you have enjoyed reading *Alves & Co.* you should enjoy reading the other books by Eça de Queiroz which we have published:

The City and the Mountains
Cousin Bazilio
The Crime of Father Amaro
The Maias
The Mandarin (and Other Stories)
The Relic
The Tragedy of the Street of Flowers

Books written by Eça de Queiroz's contemporary Mário de Sá-Carneiro might also be of interest:

Lúcio's Confession
The Great Shadow (and Other Stories)

These books can be bought from your local bookshop or online retailer or direct from Dedalus, either online or by post. Please write to **Cash Sales, Dedalus Limited, 24-26, St Judith's Lane, Sawtry, Cambs, PE28 5XE.** For further details of the Dedalus list please go to our website www.dedalusbooks.com or write to us for a catalogue.

The Maias – Eça de Queiroz

Winner of PEN/Book-of-the-Month-Club Translation Prize for 2008. Winner of the Oxford-Weidenfeld Translation Prize for 2008.

Carlos is the grandson of Afonso da Maia, the last surviving member of one of Lisbon's wealthiest and most illustrious families. Carlos is good, handsome, clever, eager to contribute something to society, and yet he appears, as he himself puts it, 'to be one of those weak hearts, soft and flaccid, incapable of preserving any true emotion'. Then, one day, walking along Lisbon's grubby streets he sees a woman who seems to him like a goddess who has just stepped down from the clouds. When he finally meets the beautiful Maria Eduarda, the attraction proves to be as mutual as it is profound. In the plenitude of that love, Carlos seems, in his best friend Ega's words, 'a truly fortunate being', until Fate steps in – in the form of a grizzled, left-wing newspaper hack from Paris – and everything unravels.

"Eça de Queiroz spent eight years writing *The Maias*. This is a novel in the tradition of Flaubert or Dickens, in which de Queiroz anatomizes a society through a brilliant drama of a family's decline and downfall. Margaret Jull Costa's translation is supple, transparent and wonderfully paced. There seems to be no barrier at all between the reader and what the author intended. The novel shades from realism to romanticism, from satire to tragedy. The vigour and charm of the characters come across beautifully in this translation, and so does de Queiroz's biting, sometimes despairing view of Lisbon society in the last quarter of the nineteenth century."
Helen Dunmore, chair of the Oxford-Weidenfeld Translation Prize

£15.00 ISBN 978 1 903517 53 6 720p B. Format

The Tragedy of the Street of Flowers – Eça de Queiroz

'An unexpected bonus: the belated English publication of a work by Portugal's great but little-known novelist, Eça de Queiroz, who died 100 years ago and bears comparison with Balzac and Flaubert. *The Tragedy of the Street of Flowers* unrolls a fascinating panorama – colourful, animated and satirically observed – of 19th-century Portugal, from its mouldering provincial towns to the flashy falsities of the capital.'   Peter Kemp in *The Sunday Times Books of the Year*

'Attractive and repellent by turns, Genoveva is a splendid creation who almost achieves stature and sympathy sufficient for tragedy in a novel otherwise suffused with irony and bathos. Through her, Eça anatomises Portuguese society, cutting through its superficial elegance to the inadequacy and insecurity he discerns – with sympathy – underneath. *The Tragedy of the Street of Flowers* justifies his claim to be numbered among the great European novelists of his day.'   Paul Duguid in *The Times Literary Supplement*

'One of the greatest novelists of the novel's greatest age, Eça is also amongst the most readable due to his narrative energy, sweeping range and tart sense of humour.' Michael Kerrigan in *The Scotsman*

'A brilliant portrayal of social hypocrisy and sexual fascination.'
The Guardian

£9.99 ISBN 978 1 873982 64 8 346p B. Format

The Crime of Father Amaro – Eça de Queiroz

'*The Crime of Father Amaro* is also the best possible introduction to Portuguese literature. It is the first great realistic novel in the language; a product of the wonderful period when it seemed to be easy, all over Europe, to write novels of the highest literary quality which were also commercial successes. So it is instantly approachable, while at the same time complex and ultimately mysterious. All these riches are made available in a brand new translation.'

Tom Earle in *The London Magazine*

'This is a terrific novel, and I hardly go out on a limb in saying so. José Maria Eça de Queiroz is generally regarded as Portugal's greatest novelist, author of some half-dozen masterpieces that bear comparison with the work of his masters, Flaubert and Zola. Chronologically, *The Crime of Father Amaro* (1876) can be regarded as Eça's first novel, though he corrected and rewrote it significantly for a later edition (1880) which the distinguished translator Margaret Jull Costa uses as her copy-text. Being sadly ignorant of Portuguese, I can only say that this new translation reads fluently and, more important, makes available to a new generation a work of mesmerizing literary power. The novel's plot is as sensational now as then: A priest, prey to erotic reverie and utterly without a true clerical vocation, half seduces, half falls in love with, the daughter of his landlady. The first two-thirds of *The Crime of Father Amaro* depicts the tactics of growing desire between Amaro and Amelia. The last third charts the consequences of their illicit passion.'

Michael Dirda in *The Washington Post*

£11.99 ISBN 978 1 873982 89 1 476p B. Format

Cousin Bazilio – Eça de Queiroz

'Sauciness and scandal come as part of the enticing package in this 1878 European classic by Portugal's most celebrated 19th century writer. Cousin Bazilio might not be his best work, but it certainly drew the most attention when it was originally published, for all the wrong reasons; specifically deceitful lusts, a series of characters – some aristocratic hedonistic socialites, others colourful, aspiring servants, but all connected by a string of naughty secrets. The tale rips along at a pace that could outdo any modern soap, while the social realist side of de Queiroz shows up the hypocritical limitations laid down by society, particularly on female morality. A classic then, but distinctly alternative in every way.' *The Scotsman*

'For a book originally published in 1878, Cousin Bazilio is astonishingly modern. It reeks of petty jealousies, middle-class ennui and of smouldering, repressed sexuality. There's even one bit where nasty old Juliana is sniffing Luisa's underwear to see if she's been putting it about. No British writer of the period would come anywhere near this sort of thing.' Eugene Byrne in *Venue*

Adultery, blackmail, sentimentality and lust all come under Eça's scrutiny. Sins are scattered amid a gallery of vivid characters, central of which are the adulterous heroine, her first love, the cuckolded husband, and most importantly, the maid. This cunning portrayal of life below stairs casts a cold eye across the hypocrisy of 'respectability', recreating the sultry summer heat of Lisbon and the tensions and passions underlying both the refinements of the wealthy and the loyalty of the servants. Sheer brilliance.

The Good Book Guide

£11.99 ISBN 9781 903517 08 6 439p B. Format

The Mandarin (and other stories) – Eça de Queiroz

'Each of the four masterly stories included in the latest Eça de Queiroz volume from Dedalus – with another fine translation by Margaret Jull Costa – contains an element of fantasy.

In *'The Mandarin'*, a novella written in 1880, Teodoro, an ageing and impoverished civil servant, fantasises about becoming rich. The Devil appears before him and offers to grant his wish if Teodoro will pray for the death of a Mandarin in distant China – the French expression *tuer le mandarin* means 'to harm someone whom you know will never meet in order to gain some personal advantage and in the certain knowledge that you never will be punished'. Teodoro duly inherits a Mandarin's fortune and enters into a life of luxury, but remorse drives him to China in a futile search for the dead man's family. He returns to Lisbon haunted by the crime.

The last three short stories deal in turn with a man's obsessive love for a woman, 'a theme that runs through much of Eça's work'. 'The Idiosyncrasies of a Young Blonde Woman' was written in 1873. Macário endures years of poverty and separation from the pretty but enigmatic Luisa, but as he is about to become engaged to her, an unsettling incident crushes his romantic ideal. In 'The Hanged Man' (1885), set in Spain, Don Ruy de Cardenas falls in love with Don Alonso's wife. In a jealous rage, Alonso forces her to write a letter that will lure Ruy to his death. On his way to the 'assignation' Ruy passes Hangman's Hill, where a supernatural event brings fateful consequences. The short story 'José Matias' (1897) chronicles the long years of José's passionate love for Elisa, during which he secretly watches her window 'with extreme refinement of spirituality and devotion'.'

Alan Biggins in *The Anglo-Portuguese Society Magazine*

'A brilliant mischievous essay in fantasy chinoiserie, irreverently subverting the trope, created half a century earlier by Balzac in *La Peau de chagrin*, of the Oriental curse masquerading as a blessing. In the same Dedalus collection of Eça's short fiction lies a late gem, 'José Matias', a love story told at a funeral by a Hegelian philosopher, in which the issue of the narrator's own relationship with reality adds a comically ambiguous layer to the tale.'

Jonathan Keates in *The Times Literary Supplement*

£7.99 ISBN 978 1903517 80 2 176p B. Format

The City and the Mountains – Eça de Queiroz

'The Portuguese Dickens, Eça de Queiróz (who spent almost 15 years as consul in Newcastle and Bristol), left this last novel behind on his death in 1900. As timely now as then, it follows – with a smart balance of satire, irony and lyric grace – the progress of a rich brat who quits the city to find fulfilment in rural life. Trustafarian Jacinto grows up in the stifling lap of luxury at 202 Champs-Elysées: an address to die for, and he almost does, smothered by the hi-tech gadgetry of the 1890s. Then, after a summons back to the family estate in Portugal, he leaves Paris for a radical makeover as nature-loving country gent. The narrator's wry tone, well caught in Margaret Jull Costa's translation, captures all the ambivalence of Jacinto's path as the retired decadent turns virtuous squire and grows "positively dull" as a result.'   Boyd Tonkin in *The Independent*

'A classic in its native Portugal, this English translation of Queiroz's posthumous novel tells the story of Jacinto, a 30-something Parisian who makes a tortuous train journey through France and Spain to his homeland only to find all his possessions have disappeared in transit. A story of magic and satire unfolds.'

Alex Donohue in *The Big Issue*

£9.99 ISBN 978 1 903517 71 0 238p B. Format

Lúcio's Confession – Mário de Sá-Carneiro

'Written in 1913 this is a thoroughly decadent story of an unusual ménage à trois which ends in a killing. It's filled with poets and artists and those special problems that sensitive people have ('Do you hear that music? It's like a symbol of my life: a wonderful melody murdered by a terrible, unworthy performer.') The last word on this magnificent period piece – bejewelled and opiated and splendidly over the top – belongs to one of its characters: "It seems more like the vision of some brilliant onanist than reality." '

Phil Baker in *The Sunday Times*

'Febrile, intense and innovative.'

Nicholas Lezard in *The Guardian*

'An enigmatic love triangle riddled with madness and jealousy, set in fin de siècle Paris and Lisbon, and its translation reopens a rich vein of fantasy.' Christopher Fowler in *Time Out*

'It is, in this sparkling new translation by Margaret Jull Costa, a fabulous testament to fin de siècle Paris – the story of an enigmatic and unusual ménage à trois, with a strong homoerotic subtext, set in a world of fantasy and madness.' Keith Richmond in *Tribune*

£8.99 ISBN 978 1 873982 80 8 121p B. Format